# Fabulous Beasts

# Fabulous Beasts

## Malcolm Ashman

Text by
## Joyce Hargreaves

## The Overlook Press
Woodstock • New York

**For Michael – 2.4.78**

First published in the United States in 1997 by
The Overlook Press, Peter Mayer Publishers, Inc.
Lewis Hollow Road
Woodstock, New York 12498

Editor  Helen Williams
Designer  Paul Skellett at Keane Design Associates
Art Director  John Strange
Editorial Director  Pippa Rubinstein

**Library of Congress Cataloging-in-Publication Data**

Ashman, Malcolm
Fabulous beasts / Malcolm Ashman ; text by
Joyce Hargreaves
1. Animals, Mythical.  I. Hargreaves, Beryl Joyce,
1932—
II. Title.
GR825.A85   1997   398.24'54—dc21   96-49488   CIP

ISBN:  0-87951-816-2 (hardback edition)
ISBN:  0-87951-779-4 (paperback edition)

Printed in Slovenia

First American Edition
1 3 5 7 9 8 6 4 2

# ontents

## Introduction 6

# Introduction

*Fabulous Beasts have enchanted and intrigued humankind from the earliest times. This book explores the curious fascination that we have for the strange, powerful and mysterious creatures that roam through the jungle of our imaginations.*

Imagination is a basic element in our makeup. It enables us to use the mental faculty of forming images or concepts of objects not present to the senses and is closely linked to the subjective state of fantasy – the faculty of inventing images. Imagination allows us to explore the ever-expanding realm of possibilities that cannot be seen unless it is present, when it can then be transferred into visual form by artistic representation. When Fabulous Beasts are created, forms found in nature are interchanged in part or completely, mixed or set apart, expanded or contracted to become creatures whose antecedents are not in doubt but whose final shape must be considered to be imaginary.

A painting, drawing or sculpture of a fabulous or composite beast can engender an emotional or other bodily response on the part of the viewer whose behaviour can be influenced by the image. When particular emotions such as fear or horror are needed to keep the uninitiated out of a temple, what better symbol could be erected over the portal than a Medusa head with her lolling tongue, boar's tusks and writhing snakes for hair.

The conscious putting together of different animals in this way, enables the feelings that the image engenders to be expressed more fully than was previously possible. In preliterate societies and even today's society, as can be seen on television, visual imagery is used to carry coded information.

People, either consciously or unconsciously, transform objects into a myriad of symbols which constitute an international language transcending the normal limits of communication.

This language is a code that must be broken to be understood, for it makes possible the perception of fundamental relationships between seemingly diverse and unrelated forms.

The zoology of fantasy has been with us from the very beginning of civilized existence. The earliest clear depictions of imaginary beasts came from sculptural reliefs and writing on clay tablets found in the ancient Near East. Tablets from Ninevah, the centre of the Assyrian empire, portrayed a creation myth – the *Enuma Elish* – that featured one of the best known fabulous creatures, the Dragoness Tiamat and her death at the hands of the God Marduk.

Other major written sources are found later in the works of Ctesias, Herodotus, Wang Fu and others up to the fifth century BC and in *Historia Naturalis (Natural History)* written by Gaius Plinius Secundus – or Pliny the Elder – in the first century AD. All these works influenced an anonymous author, now known as the Physiologus, who wrote a serious book on natural history upon which most of the medieval Bestiaries were founded. Although a number of the creatures included in his work and the Bestiaries actually exist, there were also those who were fabulous beasts, known to us only through myths and traveller's tales.

Many of the myths and Bestiaries were created in an attempt to adapt esoteric, philosophic or religious teachings to a simpler form so that they could be understood. Thus a Bestiary advocates caution in dealing with Sirens whose pretty voices lead men into licentious behaviour, while Pegasus, the winged horse, symbolizes the struggle to attain higher things.

This book is divided into four different sections, each one describing a different type of fabulous creature. First, the birds – some, like the Phoenix, the spirit of immortality, are world famous while others such as Blodeuedd who was transformed into an owl because of her wickedness, are less well known.

Dragons need hardly any introduction: they are the primary movers in creation myths; the guardians of treasure; the rain bringers; they can be as large as a mountain or as small as a worm. They are unique.

When a fabulous creature is partially human, another element – intelligence – is added to the original symbolism of the beast. For example, the Sphinx's human head is the intelligence that controls the force of its leonine body.

The last section describes animals whose natural biological shape has been altered beyond recognition. Here is the Hippogryph, a second generation hybrid, with a Griffin (part eagle, part lion) for its father and a mare for its mother; the Water Horse (part fish, part stallion); and the fearsome Peryton which is a deer with bird-like features.

*The invisible world of the imagination is brought into reality in this book. As the pages turn, this fabulous zoo of beasts is spectacularly revealed in all its glory of flashing tusks and talons, gleaming scales and soft feathers.*

# Chapter 1  BIRDS

Fabulous birds with their powers of flight are symbols of the soul, the spirit or the force of the elements. They are also instruments of communication and can be messengers, informants and escorts.

The Rainbird brings water to parched land; the Simurgh creates fertility by scattering seed, while the Heavenly Cock awakens the world each morning to greet the rising sun.

On a higher level, the Phoenix gives promise of immortality and resurrection, and in Egypt it was thought that upon the death of the physical body, the soul, or *Ba*, leaves in the shape of a bird – the Soul Bird.

In some of the world's creation myths, it is a bird who is the creator. One Egyptian myth records that in the beginning, when there was only chaos, the Nile Goose appeared out of nowhere and laid the Cosmic Egg from which the whole world emerged.

'*...Beware the Jujub bird and shun*
*The frumious Bandersnatch!...*'
Lewis Carroll, *Through the Looking Glass*

#  Nile Goose

According to the creation myths of ancient Egypt, the universe was flooded in silence during the time of non-being, until the great primeval spirit The Nile Goose came out of nowhere and, with her raucous cry broke the calm; it was then that the Great Chatterer or Cackler, as the goose was known, laid the Cosmic Egg. Egyptian priests reinterpreted the concept of a goose into that of a gander, yet it is clearly the female who cackles at the laying of her egg.

In some myths, it is said that the egg cracked open to reveal the sun god Amen-Ra, in others it was the whole world that emerged. Some sources state that the egg contained a bird of light but the authors of the Ancient Egyptian *Books of the Dead* realized that air was the first thing to be expelled from the egg.

Although the Nile Goose was a bird of the waters, she was also a solar bird and a symbol of love. A later European development turned her into a 'silly goose' and an emblem of stupidity but Ovid remarked that the goose was 'wiser than the dog'. Some tattered remnants of the Nile Goose's former glory can be seen today in the pantomime goose who lays a golden egg.

# Simurgh

In Persian folklore the Simurgh is the monarch of all birds and the most long-lived. She is a gigantic iridescent creature that lives, behind veils of light and dark, on inaccessible peaks in the Alburz mountains to the north of what is now Iran. When the Simurgh flies home, to the land where the sacred Haoma plant grows, her vast open wings are like a mist over the mountains. The tree where she alights is immortal and carries the seeds of all the wild plants of the earth. When she alights on the tree, the weight of her body shakes its branches, scattering down all the seeds that are ripening there.

This fertility spirit is the wisest of all birds, for not only can she speak and understand all languages but also knows everything that has happened in the past, is happening now, and that which is yet to come; she is both an oracle and a protector, a benefactress of man.

Early depictions of the Simurgh, also known as a Senmurv show a creature that is a cross between a bird and a dog, and resembles a griffin; she represents the elemental link between heaven and earth. Later Persian depictions of the Simurgh make her much more like a bird with only the head, teeth and paws of a dog as well as the ability to suckle her young. Her bejewelled feathers are especially prized, for just one touch of them will instantly cure any sickness. Flaubert, the nineteenth-century French author, lowered the bird's status by representing her as an attendant of the Queen of Sheba. He described the Simurgh as having metallic orange-gold feathers, four wings, a vulture's talons, a long peacock's tail and a small silver-coloured head with human features.

The Simurgh once found an abandoned baby whose hair was white as driven snow – considered by his parents to be ill-omened. She took him to her eyrie and cared for him throughout his childhood. When he left to return home, she plucked out one of her jewel-like feathers and gave it to him. The lad was able to claim his birthright, and the knowledge and wisdom he acquired from the great bird made him an illustrious leader.

## Roc

Marco Polo's *Book of Travels* and the *Arabian Nights* both described the Roc or Rukh bird, the mythological bird of Arabia. It was shaped like an eagle and was so immense that it blotted out the sun. The Roc could carry an elephant in its claws which it would kill by flying to a great height then dropping the unfortunate creature to crash to its death on the rocks below. Its wingspan was forty paces across and its feathers were as big as palm leaves; the wind was the rush of its wings and its flight was lightning. According to Arabic tradition, the Roc never lands on earth, only on the mountain Qaf, the centre of the world.

In the *Arabian Nights*, the adventurer Sinbad was stranded in a Roc's nest on top of a mountain where he found an egg as large as 148 hen's eggs. When the adult bird returned to its nest, Sinbad left his confinement by lashing himself to the Roc's leg with his turban, without the bird even noticing him. He flew with it so high into the sky that he lost sight of earth. Eventually, he was able to escape when the Roc flew near another island.

# Heavenly Cock

The cock is the tenth symbolic animal of the Twelve Terrestrial Branches of the Chinese Zodiac. The most famous of these birds is the Heavenly Cock, sometimes known as the Bird of the Dawn. It is a golden-plumed bird with three legs, who perches on the top of the great Fu-sang tree which towers above the clouds. All roosters are descended from the Heavenly Cock and it sires chicks with red combs who answer its song every morning.

This lordly bird crows loudly three times a day. The first time is early in the morning when the sun first appears over the horizon. It shakes the heavens and stirs mankind from its sleep. The second is when the sun stands high in the sky; it heralds the appearance of the Red Cock, a solar creature who is invoked as a protection against fire. It symbolises male courage and vigilance; it also represents October, when preparations for war are made. The third time that the Heavenly Cock crows is when the sun sinks in the west.

In funeral rites the Heavenly Cock was employed to ward off evil spirits as the Chinese for 'cock' sounds the same as 'fortune'. A white Cock is also solicited as a protection against ghosts.

# Rainbird

In some parts of China, drought is common and farmers, whose livelihood depended on the fertility of the land, felt that the Rain Dragons required help to bring the much needed rain. The one-legged Shang Yang, or Rainbird, was the answer to their prayers – for birds, with their powers of flight, were regarded as communicators between heaven and earth.

When rain was required, it is said the farmers would send for an aged sorcerer who had tamed a Rainbird and carried it about on his arm. When the pair arrived, the Shang Yang would draw up the water from the surrounding rivers with its beak and expel it as fine rain onto the thirsty fields.

One myth concerning the Rainbird tells how it helped the Prince of Ch'i's subjects when their land was threatened by floods, another perennial Chinese problem. During the Prince's reign, the Rainbird flew down before the royal throne hopping about on its single leg and flapping its wings wildly. This alarmed the Prince so much that he sent a messenger to Confucius asking for his advice. Confucius foretold that the Rainbird would cause vast areas of the Prince's kingdom to flood. This news gave him time to take protective measures by building banks and dams and when the floods came, his precautions saved many lives.

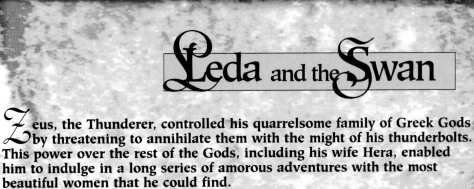

# Leda and the Swan

Zeus, the Thunderer, controlled his quarrelsome family of Greek Gods by threatening to annihilate them with the might of his thunderbolts. This power over the rest of the Gods, including his wife Hera, enabled him to indulge in a long series of amorous adventures with the most beautiful women that he could find.

One day Zeus, looking down from his high citadel at Olympus, caught sight of Leda, the comely wife of King Tyndareus of Sparta. The Thunderer was an adept in the art of metamorphosis; he had the power to transform himself into the shape of any bird or animal and would use this transposition to further his amorous ambitions. Abandoning the dignity of his regal position yet again, Zeus adopted the guise of a swan pursued by an eagle. He took refuge in Leda's bosom as she sat beside the river Eurotas and, still in the form of a swan, ravished her.

In due process of time, she laid an egg from which were hatched the twins Castor and Polyduces, and Helen whose beauty was the cause of the Trojan wars. Leda was also known as the Goddess Nemesis – the Moon Goddess in the form of a nymph.

# Stymphalian Birds

The Stymphalian Birds were also known as 'Strong-Beaked Arabian Birds' because they originally lived in Arabia and their beaks could pierce a metal breastplate as if it were made of butter; they were bronze-coloured, the size of cranes and resembled ibises. They bred and multiplied in such numbers in the Arabian desert that the land became devastated. A traveller crossing those scorching wastes had to take care that one of these birds did not fly at him, transfixing his breast with its powerful beak, for they were killers of men. Arabian hunters would wear protective cuirasses of plaited bark to trap the deadly beak giving the hunter time to wring the bird's neck. Flocks of these lethal birds migrated from Arabia to the Stymphalian marshes, near Stymphalus in Ancient Greece.

When Heracles, renowned in Greek mythology for his strength and prowess, went to the Oracle at Delphi to ask for her counsel, the Pythoness, a prophetess, advised him to serve Eurystheus King of Mycenae for twelve years and perform whatever labours might be set for him. Heracles agreed to this and his nephew Iolus shared in the labours as his charioteer.

The Sixth Labour imposed on Heracles by Eurystheus was to remove or destroy the countless brazen-beaked, man-killing birds who were roosting on the Stymphalian marshes. Here they bred, and killed both men and animals not only by using their beaks but also by discharging a shower of hard bronze feathers at them and emitting a poisonous excrement on the land, blighting all the crops. There were too many birds on the marsh for Heracles and Iolas to kill all at once and the marsh itself was not firm enough to walk on, nor passable by boat.

As Heracles stood hesitantly on the edge of the Stymphalian marsh considering the best way to perform this labour, the Goddess Athene – his constant ally – appeared before him holding a pair of bronze castanets made by Hephaestus, the Blacksmith of the Gods. These she gave to Heracles who then stood high up on a spur of Mount Cyllene, and crashed the castanets together, making such a din that the terrified birds flew up in a great flock. Heracles and Iolas shot down scores of them as they sheered off towards the Isle of Ares in the Black Sea and the pestilent creatures were never seen again on the Stymphalian marshes.

# Phoenix

The Phoenix is a universal symbol of resurrection and immortality, of long life and agelessness. The word *phoenix* in Greek means both 'a palm tree' and 'the colour purple' and most representations of this magnificent bird show that it is reddish-purple in colour with a golden band around its neck; other portraits show jewel-like plumage that is coloured red, gold and blue. It is larger than an eagle and far more graceful, and also has certain features of a pheasant. The home of the Phoenix is Arabia where it lives alone in a sacred wood and feeds only on pure air. It lives a solitary life for there is only one Phoenix alive in the world, at any one time.

The Phoenix is supposed to live for over 500 years, although Pliny wrote that it survives for 1,000. When the time comes for it to die, it fills its wings with myrrh, laudanum, nard, cassia and cinnamon, and flies with them to Phoenicia. Here the Phoenix selects the tallest palm tree that it can find and builds a nest out of the aromatic herbs on top of the tree. It sits on its nest singing a song of rare beauty until the sun ignites the nest and burns both bird and nest to ashes. But then, from the ashes, creeps a small worm which grows into a new young Phoenix. When it is strong enough, the fledgling gathers up the remains of its parent, places them inside a ball of myrrh and flies with the ball to Heliopolis in Egypt, the City of the Sun, followed at a respectful distance by a flight of birds. When the young Phoenix has laid the ashes of the old Phoenix on an altar in the city, its duty to its parent is finished, and it wings back to its home until it is time for it too to die.

In Egypt, the Arabian Phoenix is known as the Bennu. The Bennu is the 'Bird of the Sun' who represents the sun dying in its own fire every night to rise again in the morning. Illustrations of the bird in *The Book of The Coming Forth into Day*, usually known as *The Book of the Dead*, show a grey or multicoloured heron who utters the first sound at daybreak, calling the world back to life. It comes from the Isle of Fire in the Underworld, bringing the vital 'Hike', or life force, that is desired by all.

The Chinese form of the Phoenix is the Feng Hwang, the vermilion bird. It is the chief of all birds and is one of the four spiritually endowed Chinese creatures; the other three are the Tortoise, the Ch'i-lin and the Dragon. There are both male and female birds; the female bird Hwang is Yin, lunar and represents beauty, delicacy of feeling and peace, for the Feng Hwang is never seen in times of war; Feng the male is Yang, solar and the bird of fire. When the Feng Hwang appears with the Dragon, the symbol of the Emperor, it is entirely feminine and the symbol of the Empress.

The traditional description of this exalted bird gives it the head of a cock, the back of a swallow, its wings are the wind, its tail is formed of trees and flowers, and its feet are the earth. The Feng Hwang is a bringer of good luck and will not harm a living thing; it will not even tread on grass. Its sweet song can sometimes be heard, especially if anyone nearby is playing the flute.

# Blodeuedd

The story of Blodeuedd, the flower maiden, is one of eleven medieval Welsh tales to be found in *The Mabinogion*.

Lleu, the bastard son of Aranrhod, daughter of Dôn, was raised by his uncle Gwydyon. But when the boy reached manhood, Aranrhod said,

'I will swear a fate on the boy; he shall never have a wife of the race that now inhabits the earth.'

'You always were a spiteful woman,' replied Gwydyon, 'but all the same, he will have a wife.'

Thereupon Gwydyon brought Lleu before Math, Lord of Gwynedd, and the pair agreed to use their magical powers to create a wife for Lleu out of flowers. The two magicians took the flowers of broom, oak and meadowsweet, and from them conjured up a beautious maiden and gave her the name Blodeuedd.

After the wedding feast, the couple retired to the cantrev of Dinoding and settled there content, until one day, when Lleu was away from home. Goronwy the Staunch, Lord of Penllyn passed by in pursuit of a stag; by the time the noble lord had killed his prey, night was closing in and Blodeuedd commanded her servants to invite him to spend the night in her castle. That evening as all were feasting, Blodeuedd and Goronwy gazed deeply into each other's eyes and were filled with love for each other. Goronwy said to Blodeuedd,

'Be affectionate to your husband, and try to find out how I may bring about his death!'

When Lleu returned home and retired to bed with his wife, he spoke to her but she did not answer him, then a second time, again there was no reply.

'What ails you?' he asked. Blodeuedd feigned grief and answered,

'I fear that you will die before I do.'

'I will be hard to destroy.'

'Please tell me why. I will safeguard your secret.'

'Gladly my beloved. I can only be killed by a spear manufactured by a man working on it during Mass on Sundays. I cannot be killed inside a house or outdoors, on horse or on foot.'

'Then how can you be killed?'

'Make a bath for me on the river with a roof over the bathtub. Place a goat beside the tub and if I stand with one foot on the goat and one on the edge of the tub, then I can be slain.'

'Thank God! You will never be killed,' said she, and forthwith sent the information to Goronwy, who set to work on his weapon.

At the end of a year Goronwy had finished making the spear and Blodeuedd said to her husband,

'Show me how you could be destroyed. If I prepare the bath, will you demonstrate how it can be done?' Lleu did as she asked and balanced himself between the goat and the tub. Then Goronwy rose up from behind a mound of earth and pierced him in the side with his poisoned spear. Lleu gave a terrible scream when he felt the pain and flew up into the air in the form of an eagle.

Meanwhile Gwydyon, who had a feeling of foreboding, set forth to visit his nephew. With the aid of his magic powers, it was not long before he found the eagle and changed Lleu back into human form. Lleu was a piteous sight for he was nothing but skin and bone but, with the help of the good physicians of Gwynedd, he was healed before the end of the year. Lleu then slew Goronwy by impaling him with a skilful throw of his spear. Thereafter he was known as Lleu Skilful Hand. When Blodeuedd heard the news, she fled. But Gwydyon overtook her and, grim-faced, said,

'Death is too good a fate for you! From henceforward you will never show your face to the light of day. You will become an owl and always fear other birds for they will be hostile to you.' Then Blodeuedd flew away to retain the form of an owl forever.

# Chapter 2

# DRAGONS & SERPENTS

The Dragon was the symbol of the Earth Goddess and represented her powers of fertility and wisdom. In ancient times, the Dragon and the serpent were closely linked; even today some Dragons are known as Worms and are completely snake-like without legs or wings. The Greek words *drakon* and *draco* were used to describe a large snake; 'Dragon' is derived from both of them.

The word *drakon* comes from a verb meaning 'to see' or 'to watch' and Dragons have great reputations as guardians of wisdom, treasure and the virtue of young maidens entrusted to them. Nowadays a conscientious chaperone may be described as a Dragon, an unconscious tribute to her vigilance.

Why then, today, is the Dragon regarded as the apotheosis of evil? In war, when one community is conquered by another, the gods of the loser are either assimilated into the victor's culture or stigmatized as devils. This is what happened to the Dragon. Even in the Greek myths, it is clear that the religion of the Earth Goddess was being destroyed. Apollo slew the Python, prophetess of the Oracle of Delphi, and Heracles killed the watchful guardian Dragon Ladon, the son of Mother Earth. In the Old Testament, the serpent in the Garden of Eden was portrayed as a snake with a human head, the sign of the Earth Goddess. The Dragon who was once a great symbol of fertility has now acquired an undeservedly evil reputation; but not in every country, for the Dragons of the Orient still retain their virtues of wisdom, fecundity and benevolence.

> *'...Beware the Jabberwock, my son!*
> *The jaws that bite, the claws that catch!...'*
> Lewis Carroll, *Through the Looking Glass*

# Tiamat

The account of the Babylonian creation epic *Enuma Elish* was discovered in the form of a long poem on seven tablets, excavated on the site of Ninevah, near the modern day Iraqi town of Mosul. These tablets date from the second millennium BC and, when translated, the story of the Dragoness Tiamat was unfolded.

In the beginning there was nothing, no land, Gods or mankind but only two elements – Apsu, the male spirit of fresh water and the abyss, and Tiamat, the female spirit of salt water and chaos. Eventually the union of these two was cursed, rather than blessed, by their numerous progeny. As the numbers of their children, known as the Gods, increased, Apsu became more and more enraged by their boisterous ways and sought to destroy them. The Gods, sensing their peril, killed him before he could strike.

...

Tiamat lived on in her own element of salt water, brooding over the death of her husband and plotting revenge. She decided to make war against the Gods and produced reinforcements for the battle to come by spawning eleven monsters; these were the viper, the shark, the scorpion man, the storm demon, the great lion, the dragon, the mad dog and the four nameless ones. It was a fearsome sight to see the serpentine dragoness, protected by a hide that weapons could not pierce, surrounded by her army of demonic creatures.

The Gods were terrified but one, Marduk, was her only adversary who was not afraid. Armed with a bow and arrows, a mace, lightning and a net of the four winds, Marduk advanced to meet his deadly enemy. There was an epic struggle between Tiamat and Marduk. Eventually Marduk seized his chance, spread out his net and caught her in it. As she opened her mouth to swallow him, Marduk drove in an evil wind so that she could not close her lips. Then he was able to shoot his arrows at her innards and split her heart in two. He felled Tiamat's body and stood triumphantly upon it. Marduk was now Supreme Lord and set about creating our familiar world. He divided Tiamat's body into two parts, which became the upper and lower firmaments – the sky and the land. The Gods and their enemies agreed to live in peace providing they had servants, so Marduk cut off the head one of Tiamat's advisers and from his blood fashioned humanity to act as slaves to the Gods.

# Azhi Dahaki

*I*n Persian mythology Angra Mainyu, the Father of Lies, created the dragon Azhi Dahaki to rid the world of righteousness. This fearsome monster had three heads, three jaws and six eyes; his body was filled with lizards, scorpions and other foul reptiles. If he were ever cut open, these venomous creatures would infect the world.

The ancient Zoroastrian hymn *Zamyad Yasht* tells how Azhi Dahaki sought to extinguish the light of the sacred flame known as The Divine Glory. Atar, the God of Fire, ran to save the Glory but the dragon challenged the God by threatening to destroy the light of his fire forever. Atar responded by swearing to send his flames throughout the Dragon's body. In fear, Azhi Dahaki drew back but in retribution for the damage that he did to humankind, the divine hero Thraetaona bound and imprisoned him on Mount Demavend, near the Caspian Sea.

Zoroastrians believe that when the world comes to an end, Azhi Dahaki will break free from his bonds and escape from the mountain. His fury, so long repressed, will allow no interference as he attacks all creation, devouring a third of men and animals until he is killed by another great hero, the youthful Keresaspa.

# Quetzalcoatl

Quetzalcoatl, the brilliant Lord of the Morning Star, was the spirit who came forth out of the jaws of the serpent that wore the turquoise-green feathers of the Quetzal bird, just as the Morning Star rose to herald the sunrise. *Quetzaltotolin* means 'most precious bird' and gives the name Quetzalcoatl – 'most precious serpent' – to both the God and his symbol, the feathered serpent.

Quetzalcoatl came forth from within the serpent just as the Morning Star rose to herald the break of day and, by causing the sun to rise in the morning, he was worshipped by the Toltec Mexicans as the one who brought fertility to the land and light to his people. Quetzalcoatl sometimes appeared before his subjects arched across the sky, an incomparable sight with the serpent's iridescent body gleaming in the sunlight. At other times when he wanted to mingle with mortals unrecognized, he appeared as an old man with a white beard and broken walking stick or as a young man in a feathered cloak.

This God did not come empty-handed to his people. He taught them the art of agriculture – including the cultivation of the maize plant, how to dig into the earth to mine gold and precious stones, the secrets of the zodiac, and the movements of the planets and the stellar system. He was the inspiration behind poetry, learning and all works of art from the simplest sketch to the most elaborate piece of jewellery.

Quetzalcoatl was a gentle god who would not permit human sacrifice while he was visible in the sky; only flowers and fruit were allowed in his holy place. He lived a chaste and holy life until he was tempted by his sister the Moon Goddess Tlazoteotl. The Moon Goddess had four aspects. Her first was a young girl, cruel but enchanting; her second was a sensual woman with dubious morality; the third was a priestess who purified the soul; her fourth aspect was that of an ancient hag. The Goddess, in her second, most seductive aspect, plied Quetzalcoatl with strong drink and magic mushrooms. Under their hallucinatory influence, he copulated with her.

Quetzalcoatl realized that his time on Earth had come to an end, for he had defiled and condemned himself by this act. He left his palaces and travelled to the shores of the Caribbean sea where he embarked, naked, on a raft of serpent skins and sailed towards the sunrise. The sun's heat ignited the boat and Quetzalcoatl's incandescent heart flew up to join the sun. His people wait patiently for one day, they say, he will return.

# Hydra

The Hydra is described in mythology as a personification of the fertilizing powers of water. Today, because of this association with fertility, anything that is hard to destroy either by its return to life or by reproducing itself, may be called hydra-headed. One of the earliest representations of the multi-headed Hydra can be seen on a cylinder seal from Syria which dates back to the fourteenth century BC and shows the influence on Canaanite mythology of the earlier Babylonian story of the slaying of the dragoness Tiamat. It portrays part of one of the myths of the fertility god Baal and tells of his conquest over the seven-headed dragon Latan, a creature identified with the watery forces of chaos and disorder.

The Greek hero Heracles' fight with the Lernaean Hydra – his Second Labour – shows clearly this dragon's powers of renewal. The Hydra's mother was the serpent-maiden Echidne and her father was Typhon, a terrifying creature with a hundred dragon's heads sprouting from his shoulders and eyes that flashed searing flames. The Hydra herself was also an unnerving sight for she inherited some of the most fearsome characteristics of her parents. She had a prodigious dog-like body, eight or nine reptilian heads, and venomous breath that was quite lethal. One of her heads was immortal and made of gold. The Hydra of Lernaea had her lair beneath a plane tree, close by an unfathomable swamp at the source of the river Amymone. Heracles was fearless enough to penetrate this swamp and forced the Hydra to emerge from her lair by pelting her with burning arrows. Then, holding his breath in order to avoid destruction, he struck viciously at her with his great club. But he battered at her heads in vain for, as soon as one monstrous head was destroyed, two or three others grew in its place. Heracles was so incensed by his inability to destroy the creature that he called to his nephew Iolus for assistance. Iolus set a grove on fire and, to prevent new heads forming, charred each neck with a burning brand. Eventually Heracles was able to sever the remaining immortal head of the Hydra and buried it still alive and hissing under a heavy rock. He cut the carcass apart to make sure that the Lernaean Hydra could not regenerate and dipped his weapons in its gall which made the least wound from any one of them fatal.

The Bible too has its own Hydra in *The Apocrypha*. Probably the most infamous dragon in all history, this Hydra is described as being a great red dragon with seven heads, ten horns and seven crowns upon his heads. There was war in Heaven. The Dragon and his hosts fought against the Archangel of the Light Saint Michael and his angels but was unable to prevail against the forces of righteousness. Saint Michael cast the 'old serpent called the Devil and Satan which deceiveth the whole world' out of Heaven and on to the earth together with his warriors. The Dragon's open mouth was then portrayed as the door to Hell.

# Wyvern

The Wyvern is a two-legged species of serpentine dragon whose name comes from the French *wyvere* which means both 'viper' and 'life'. The French Wyvern, known as a Vouivre or Wouive, is portrayed with the head and upper body of a voluptuous woman with a ruby or garnet set between her eyes. With this jewel she is able to guide herself through the Underworld.

Wouive is the good 'Genius' who hovers protectively over the countryside and is in rapport with the underlying currents of the earth. She is 'the spirit that breathes or inspires.' The ancients represented these currents, that today we term cosmic or magnetic, by winged serpents and the Wouive represents one of these personifications.

However, the life-giving aspect of the Wyvern seems to be inverted in some western cultures, for the Wyvern that appears in some folk tales is a malign and violent predator with a fierce head, bat's wings and a tail that sometimes has an extra head on its end. It is a taker, not a giver, of life. Even the Wouive's 'Breath of Life' has been reversed, for the Wyvern is said to have poisonous and corrupt breath. Indeed, in heraldry it betokens war, pestilence, envy and viciousness.

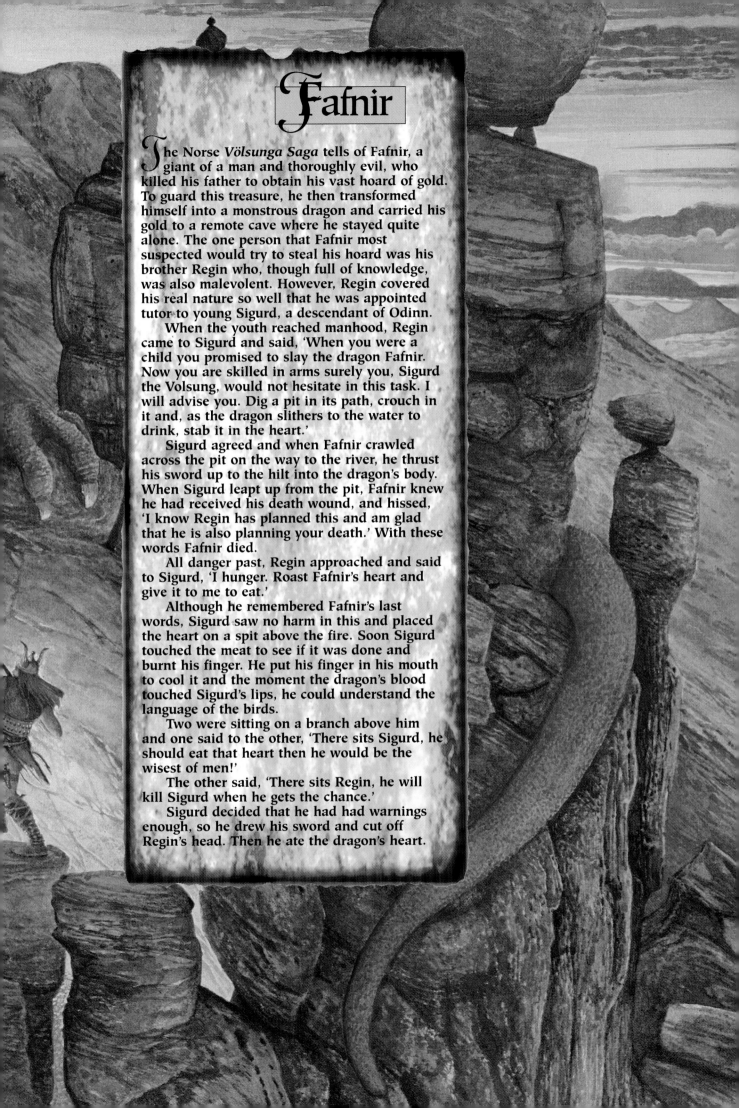

# Fafnir

The Norse *Völsunga Saga* tells of Fafnir, a giant of a man and thoroughly evil, who killed his father to obtain his vast hoard of gold. To guard this treasure, he then transformed himself into a monstrous dragon and carried his gold to a remote cave where he stayed quite alone. The one person that Fafnir most suspected would try to steal his hoard was his brother Regin who, though full of knowledge, was also malevolent. However, Regin covered his real nature so well that he was appointed tutor to young Sigurd, a descendant of Odinn.

When the youth reached manhood, Regin came to Sigurd and said, 'When you were a child you promised to slay the dragon Fafnir. Now you are skilled in arms surely you, Sigurd the Volsung, would not hesitate in this task. I will advise you. Dig a pit in its path, crouch in it and, as the dragon slithers to the water to drink, stab it in the heart.'

Sigurd agreed and when Fafnir crawled across the pit on the way to the river, he thrust his sword up to the hilt into the dragon's body. When Sigurd leapt up from the pit, Fafnir knew he had received his death wound, and hissed, 'I know Regin has planned this and am glad that he is also planning your death.' With these words Fafnir died.

All danger past, Regin approached and said to Sigurd, 'I hunger. Roast Fafnir's heart and give it to me to eat.'

Although he remembered Fafnir's last words, Sigurd saw no harm in this and placed the heart on a spit above the fire. Soon Sigurd touched the meat to see if it was done and burnt his finger. He put his finger in his mouth to cool it and the moment the dragon's blood touched Sigurd's lips, he could understand the language of the birds.

Two were sitting on a branch above him and one said to the other, 'There sits Sigurd, he should eat that heart then he would be the wisest of men!'

The other said, 'There sits Regin, he will kill Sigurd when he gets the chance.'

Sigurd decided that he had had warnings enough, so he drew his sword and cut off Regin's head. Then he ate the dragon's heart.

# Yggdrasil's Dragons

*I*n Old Norse tradition, the ash tree Yggdrasil, or the Cosmic Tree of Life, stands at 'the still point of the turning world' supporting the entire universe. Its branches overhang all the worlds and reach far into the heavens. The three great roots at the base of the tree descend into a tripartite underworld; one root twists towards the frost giants and is under their protection; one root reaches to Aesir where the Gods have their judgement seat; the third stands over Niflheim where Hel reigns as Queen of the Underworld. Underneath Hel's domain is the roaring cauldron called Nvergelmir with the dragon Nidhogg gnawing at the root from below. Nidhogg is known as 'The Dread Biter' for he actively seeks to destroy the universe with his malefic powers.

While the dragon Nidhogg is the evil that threatens the universe; Midgard's or Jornungand's Worm was the bane that afflicted the earth. The Worm lay in the seas encircling the land with its tail in its mouth, creating the oceans only to regurgitate them. If its tail were ever wrenched out of its mouth, calamity would befall the world.

The very fact that this foul worm was lying in the sea unmolested presented a challenge to the hot-tempered, red-headed Weather God Thor. He determined to smite Midgard's Worm with his fearsome hammer, which always returned to his hand when thrown. Thor persuaded the giant Hymir to take him fishing and, by baiting his strong fishing line with a succulent ox head, succeeded in hooking his adversary. In the words of Snorri Sturluson, the thirteenth-century Icelandic author:

'I can tell you this for certain: nobody ever saw a more blood-freezing sight than Thor did, as his eyes goggled down at the serpent and the Great Worm from below glared up and blew a cloud of poison. At that, they say the giant Hymir blenched, then turned yellow in his terror, what with the sea swishing into the boat and out of the boat! But Thor grabbed his hammer and flung it above his head just as Hymir fumbled for the knife he used for chopping bait and hacked Thor's fishing rod overboard! The serpent sank down into the depths of the sea.'

Thor was mortified at his failure and thumped Hymir, upending him into the sea so that all the God could see of him was the soles of his feet. Eventually Thor and Midgard's Worm met again at Ragnarok, the Doom of the Gods, where they killed each other.

# Lambton Worm

The story of Northumbria's Lambton Worm is one of the most complete and well-known of all north-east England's dragon legends. At the time of the Dragon's ominous appearance in the fifteenth century, the Lambton family were living in County Durham close by the River Wear. The Lambtons could trace their lineage back to the Saxon period and were a family of good and valorous repute, with the exception of young John Lambton. The young lord was by all accounts a wild and consummate rake who, regardless of the obligations of his high office, led an evil and dissolute life.

One Sabbath he elected to go fishing in the River Wear instead of attending church with the rest of his family. At first he was not successful, but eventually he felt a bite on the line. His satisfaction soon left him when he landed his catch for, writhing on his hook was an ugly little goggly-eyed worm with nine holes on either side of its mouth. John Lambton, in disgust, threw it into a nearby well. A passing stranger called out, 'Caught anything?'

Lambton replied, indicating the well, 'I think I've caught the Devil himself!'

The man shook his head at the repulsive creature lying in the clear water and remarked 'It tokens no good.'

That night the young lord could not sleep but tossed and turned in his tapestry-hung bed, thinking of all the sins he had committed and how bitterly he regretted them now. Next morning he sought out the family's venerable priest and in tears repented of all his crimes. The cleric blessed the young man and advised him to join the crusades 'to win the city of Our Lord out of the heathens' hands.' Lambton followed his advice and left home to fight the Saracens for seven long years.

Meanwhile, in the words of a nineteenth-century ballad:

> *...the Worm it grew and grew*
> *So lithlie and so strong,*
> *And stretched itself at morning prime*
> *An hundred yards along*
> *The river bank, and offtimes wrought*
> *Sad devastation wrong.*
>
> *Lord Lambton from his father heard,*
> *With horror and great dread,*
> *How all that battled with the worm*
> *Had foul and fatal sped;*
> *Though cut in twain, the severed parts*
> *Were quick again re-wed.*
>
> *He's boun' him to a wise woman,*
> *Ligged nigh to Chester town.*
> *"Oh! vengeance drear for all thy crimes,*
> *Lord Lambton, has come down!*
> *List, and obey, and I will strive*
> *Thy happiness to crown.*
>
> *"A coat of mail thou shalt prepare,*
> *Thigh clasps of steel also;*
> *Thy back and breast with good steel blades*
> *All studded in a row;*
> *And when the tide is ebbing fast,*
> *Into the river go.*
>
> *"Near the wormhill, where at mid-day*
> *He coils him three times round,*
> *And when the water laves thy waist*
> *Loud let the bugle sound;*
> *Stand firm, and pray Our Lady's grace*
> *To spare thee thy death-wound."*

As a fee for her wise counsel, the wise woman demanded the life of the first creature that Lambton met after his success; otherwise he would incur a curse that for nine generations no Lord of his name would die in his bed.

John Lambton followed her advice and clad in his outlandish armour stood upon a rock in the middle of the river. When he saw the Worm

wrapped around its hill, he blew his horn with all his might. The Worm uncoiled fold upon fold, slithered through the river and twined itself about the gallant knight. It tried to crush him with its poisonous embrace but the tighter the Worm coiled, the deeper the good steel blades on the armour cut its body through and through. At last great pieces of the Worm's flesh were severed and borne away by the swiftly flowing river until only its head was left glaring fiercely at the knight. Finally that too fell away and vanished.

Then Lambton raised the horn to his lips and blew a triumphant blast. His father heard the joyful sound and rushed to embrace his victorious son, quite forgetting the instruction John had given him to let his greyhound arrive first. John was horrified. How could he kill his own father? He could not. Hoping that the curse might still be averted, he blew another blast on his horn and killed the hound as it bounded towards him. All in vain. The curse came into operation and for three times three generations no Lambton died at home in his bed.

# Basilisk

The Basilisk is the king of the snakes and the absolute monarch of smaller reptiles. Its thick serpentine body is supported by bird-like legs, and its narrow, pointed head is topped by three crests. Most Basilisks are illustrated in bestiaries and early natural history books with the tuft on the top of their heads in the form of a crown, a reminder that the Basilisk is a royal creature. The name Basilisk comes from the greek word *basileus* which means king.

Although less than 1 metre long, the Basilisk is as savage as the most ferocious of dragons. This venomous beast is so destructive that its breath contaminates surrounding vegetation and even sets fire to stone. The waters of the streams where it quenches its thirst become so infected that they remain poisoned for centuries. But by far the most devastating weapons in the Basilisk's armoury are its glowing eyes; one searing glance from them is enough to kill a man instantly, hence the expression that describes a hard look as a 'Basilisk stare'. These murderous eyes are also its own downfall, for the sight of its own reflection in a mirror is enough to kill the Basilisk itself. Only two animals are capable of killing the Basilisk – the weasel, who can bite it to death, and the cock, whose crowing sends it into a fit from which it never recovers.

During the first century AD, the deserts of North Africa were reputed to be home to many of these lethal reptiles, and travellers crossing the desert often used to take a number of cockerels with them as protection against Basilisks. These travellers began to describe a very different type of Basilisk which had the head of a cock instead of that of a reptile. It was at first called a Basilcock and later a Cockatrice.

The Cockatrice's birth is very curious. It has to be born from a shell-less egg which is laid by a seven-year-old cock during the period when Sirius the Dog Star can be seen in the sky. This spherical egg must then be hatched by a toad or snake on a dung heap. The Cockatrice that emerges from the egg has eyes that resemble those of a toad but still retain their basilisk stare and it is just as destructive as the Basilisk. To the medieval Christians it represented sin and sudden death.

# Chapter 3

## HALF HUMAN

When a composite creature is partially human and part animal, bird or fish, it takes on the power and symbolism of every feature represented. Thus a Centaur combines the strength, speed and instinct of a horse with the intelligence of the human upper body, a composite creature with wings is a symbol of ascension and spiritual aspiration, while horns denote divinity and supernatural powers.

In Greek mythology, the Old Man of the Sea fathered a tribe of Mermen called Tritons, who showed their piscean origins by having fins on their bellies, scaled bodies, dolphin's tails and seaweed for hair. But it was their human brains that gave them the ability to show benevolence and a sense of obligation, although they were also lascivious and rather rough. When Poseidon drove his team of dolphins across the sea, the Tritons acted as outriders, blowing shrill blasts on their conch shells to warn everyone to keep their distance.

However, when the animal part is dominant in a Fabulous Beast, there is a lessening of the benign human characteristics. When the composition of the monster includes an animal's head upon a human body, such as the Minotaur, the domination of the baser animal forces is carried to their extreme conclusion.

*Triton – half man, half sea-creature*

# Mermaids & Mermen

The Mermaid, like the Merman, derives her name from the Anglo-Saxon word *mer* which means 'sea'. She is one of the most popular and decorative of all the fabulous beasts. The image of a creature swimming powerfully through the tumultuous surf, that is a coldly beautiful woman from the waist up and a glistening silvery fish below, has inspired artists from the earliest of times.

Some of the earliest depictions of Mermaids and Mermen were in the drawings of the Babylonian Water God Oannes or Ea. At first, pictures of this God showed a man-like creature wearing the head of a fish above his human visage, with his legs ending in a fishtail. Later sculptures figured him as a true Merman, with the upper parts of a bearded man and his lower half the muscular tail of a fish. It was said that this God had a human voice and taught his people the arts of civilization. His retinue included both Mermen and Mermaids who held vases of lifegiving water.

Early portraits and sculptures of the Mermaid show her as a Goddess; the Sumerian goddess Nin-Mah, the Mother of the Universe and the essence or heart of the sea, was often portrayed as a Mermaid; it was written that her heartbeat governed the tides and waves of the Southern Ocean. In Syria she was the Goddess Dercerto, and in Greece the Mermaid or Merrymaid was a disguise of the ancient Sea Goddess Aphrodite. It is here that she appears in her familiar form rising from the sea, carrying her attributes of a round mirror and a golden comb.

In Greek mythology, the Merman Proteus, sometimes called Nereus, was the shepherd of the flocks of the ocean and is portrayed bearing a shepherd's crook. As flowing water is constantly changing, Proteus was also able to change his shape at will. Another Sea God was Triton, also called The Old Man of the Sea. This amphibious being was very jealous of his skill at playing the conch shell and

drowned the trumpeter Misenua whose ability exceeded his own. The Old Man of the Sea was usually a peaceful deity who often assisted seafarers in trouble by blowing on his conch shell which caused even the roughest seas to subside.

Later, in medieval times Guillaume Rondelet described a type of Merman called a Monk Fish in his *Book of Sea Fishes*. The Monk Fish had a tonsured head, a scaly cowl and a robe that ended in a fish tail. It was known in China as the Hai Ho Shang, or 'Sea Buddhist Priest'. It was said to be so aggressive that it upturned junks and drowned the crew. It could only be driven away by the strong stench of burning feathers or by a member of the threatened crew performing a ritual dance. The Chinese believed that Mermen or other sea monsters with human heads were the spirits of drowned men desperate to find a human substitute to take their place.

Mermaids have reputations, like those of the Sirens, for luring men to live with them beneath the sea, especially if they are young and handsome. Sailors, who are isolated from women by their careers and are particularly susceptible, say that they have seen them sitting on rocks at the site of such dangerous places as reefs and whirlpools, singing to themselves, coaxing the unwary to come closer. The wind is the Mermaid's song and in stormy weather she can be seen dancing on the waves. Then sailors should beware, for a person soon to die by drowning is said to see a mermaid frolicking in the water in anticipation of fresh company. In northern France, Breton mermaids sing enchantingly as they comb their long hair, and their great joy in life is to rescue young shipwrecked mariners and care for them. However, they are very possessive and will never let their charges leave them.

Mermaids can sometimes be captured and kept for the knowledge that they can give to humans, particularly their understanding of herbal lore and the ability to prophesy by foretelling the advent of catastrophes, tidal waves and storms. The greatest wish of a Mermaid is to gain a human soul but only rarely can she achieve this, for she must first transform herself into an aeriel spirit and cause no harm for 300 years.

# Sphinx

The giant sculpture of the Sphinx at Giza in Egypt is one of the oldest representations of a fabulous beast still in existence. It was originally thought to have been constructed by the Pharoah Chephren about 2700 BC, but as a result of recent geological surveys of it and the surrounding rock formations, the Sphinx is now considered to be far older than this. This mysterious and enigmatic sculpture can be seen on the Giza plateau looking east over the Nile; it has the recumbent body of a lion and the head of a man.

According to an inscription of the Egyptian eighteenth dynasty, the Sphinx represents three Gods: Hor-em-akhen, Horus of the Horizon; Kepri, the sacred scarab capable of recreating itself; and Atum, the God who symbolizes the setting and the rising sun. In this context, the Sphinx is a symbol of resurrection but on a more physical level, the juxtaposition of a human head and an animal's body shows that the Sphinx is not to be considered as a real animal but as a being endowed with special powers characteristic of both humans and animals. The human head is the intelligence that controls the force of the lion's body and the Sphinx, with its head carved into the likeness of a Pharoah, represents the physical and spiritual powers that are incarnate in the ruler.

There are statues of a number of different types of Sphinx to be seen in Egypt. The two most important are the Criosphinx, who has a lion's body and the head of a ram. It represents silence and was worshipped as a symbol of Amon whose soul was believed to be enshrouded in it. The other is the Hieracosphinx who has the head of a falcon and represents the solar power of the God Horus.

Not every Egyptian Sphinx is masculine; there are some that have female features, possibly representing the Goddess Hathor. But there can be no doubt about the femininity of the Greek Sphinx as the head is clearly that of a woman and her lion's body generally carries human breasts. She is described as having the head of a woman, the body of a lion, the tail of a serpent and the wings of an eagle. She is the symbol of destruction, the enemy of humankind and also the supreme embodiment of the enigma that is forever beyond human understanding.

The Sphinx, who was reputed to be the daughter of the serpent monster Echidne and Typhon, was sent by the Gods to the Greek city of Thebes in Bocotia to punish it for the crimes of its king. She sat on a clifftop outside the city and waylaid travellers who passed by with demands for an answer to her riddle:

'What creature with only one voice walks on four legs in the morning, two at noon and three in the evening, and is weakest when it has most?'

Those who were unable to answer her riddle were promptly throttled, which may be the reason why the Greek word for Sphinx now means 'strangler'.

Oedipus fled to Thebes in an effort to escape from the prophecy that he would kill his father and marry his mother. Not unexpectedly, he was accosted by the Sphinx who demanded an answer to her riddle.

'Man,' he replied, 'he crawls when he is a baby, stands upright in his prime and leans on his staff when he is old.' The Sphinx, mortified by his correct answer, threw herself to her death on the rocks below.

In memory of this Oedipan monster, the Greeks portrayed the Sphinx on military ensigns and flags, and effigies of her were used for funerary purposes. It is thought that the image of the Greek Sphinx was derived either from figures of the human-headed lion which infiltrated from Egypt or from a representation of the winged Moon Goddess of Thebes.

Astrologers consider that the Sphinx is an astrological symbol and a calendar beast. The female head corresponds to Virgo the virgin, and the body to Leo the lion. The Sphinx that is depicted with a human face, a bull's body, a lion's legs and the wings of an eagle, represents the fixed signs of the zodiac – Aquarius, Taurus, Leo and Scorpio.

# Centaur

The Centaur is one of the most ancient of the Fabulous Beasts. In Assyria, illustrations of the Centaur dating from the second millennium BC have been found, and also from the third millennium BC in India, where Centaurs are said to be derived from the Gandharvas who, in Vedic mythology, drove the horses of the sun. Centaurs are portrayed with the head and body of a man from the navel upwards, set upon the body and legs of a horse. However, there are a number of different types of Centaur. 'The Physiologus', the anonymous author of a book that was the ancestor of medieval bestiaries, described Onocentaurs as having a human head, arms and torso and the lower parts of an ass. The Apotharni were a tribe of half-horse, half-human creatures whose females were bald and bearded, and the Scythian Ipopodes were human apart from their equine legs and feet. Occasionally the Centaur's lower body can be that of a lion or some other wild beast.

In Greek mythology, the Magnesian Centaurs were fathered by Centaurus, born of the cloud woman Nephele. Though of noble appearance, they were greedy, arrogant and lecherous. The mating of the God Chronus and sea nymph Philyra produced the immortal Centaur Chiron, who fathered another completely different tribe of Centaurs. This race was sober, learned and studious.

Chiron, King of the Centaurs, was described as the justest of beings and 'The Beast Divine'. Renowned for his wisdom and skill in the arts of medicine, music and archery, he taught these skills to the hero Achilles, and to Aesculapius, the son of Apollo. One day, a number of Centaurs, who were fleeing from Heracles, took refuge with Chiron. A poison-tipped arrow from Heracles' bow missed its target and stuck in Chiron's knee. He retired in agony to his cave, yet could not die. To escape from his everlasting torment Chiron surrendered his immortality to Prometheus. Zeus fixed his image in the sky as the constellation Sagittarius.

# Pan & Satyrs

When mankind lived a much simpler existence, growing corn and tending their flocks, it was to the awe-inspiring shepherd's god Pan that he prayed. This wild, free spirit of the hills was the offspring of a nymph and Hermes, the messenger of the Gods, who had seduced her while he was transformed into a goat. The child of this union looked very strange for he had horns, a tail and goat legs, which so frightened his mother that she ran away from him in panic, a fear that Pan inspires in all who do not know him intimately. However, Hermes was delighted with his son and often carried him up to Olympus to amuse the Gods.

It has also been said that Pan, the Greek Shepherd God of Hellenistic times, was a far older god than Hermes and was Zeus's foster brother. Possibly he was confused with the Satyrs who also had goat-like hairy skin, tails, small horns on their heads and monkey-like human faces. Long ago they were the resident spirits of specific localities where they animated and personified the fruitfulness of the land. Pictorially the shape of the Satyr changed as it came under the influence of the type that is associated with Pan. The lower half of the Satyr became completely goat-like and he became the symbol not only of fecundity, but also of aggressive sexuality.

The Satyrs were usually figures of fun but their sins were venal rather than mortal. They would chase and try to rape unsuspecting nymphs; the exceptions were the nereids, or water nymphs, whom the Satyrs left entirely alone as they were frightened of water. The Greek Satyrs were often depicted as attendants of the jovial and tipsy Silenus, the tutor of Dionysus. They were usually drunk, cowardly, boastful womanizers, and their names show some of the facets of their characters and appearance, for example: Simos, 'Snubnose'; Posthon, 'Prick'; Hybris, 'Insolence' and Komos, 'Revelry'. The Satyrs represent lust, permissiveness and the powers of untamed nature, but they were relatively harmless and ridiculous, often behaving in an absurd and vulgar manner.

Unlike the Satyrs, Pan had the face of an intelligent young man and was not totally mischievous but took an interest in the well-being of the shepherds and their flocks. Pan loved the timbered mountain slopes, snowy ridges and verdant pastures; he was playful, energetic and lecherous, claiming to have seduced all the maenads and various nymphs including Echo. The chaste Pitys managed to escape his advances by changing herself into a fir tree, a branch of which Pan wore as a chaplet on his head in remembrance of her.

His most famous rejection was by the nymph Syrinx. Many a time, in the shady woodland, this nymph eluded the advances of the Satyrs for she was a follower of the chaste Artemis. Pan also tried to woo Syrinx with sweet words and endearments but she scorned him and fled through the forest, pursued by her lustful suitor. When the river halted her flight, she begged the nereids to save her and, as Pan reached out for her, he found that she had been transformed into a handful of marsh reeds. As he stood sadly holding the reeds, a wind blew through them making a sweet plaintive sound. The God was enraptured,

'At least, nymph,' he cried, 'we can talk together!' He bound unequal lengths of the reeds together and made the first syrinx or pan pipes.

At one time, the Gods of Mount Olympus fled to Egypt in terror and assumed animal disguises, in order to escape the burning breath of the monster Typhon who had launched an attack on them. Pan decided to change completely into a goat, but was so distracted by his efforts to effect a metamorphosis, that he fell into the river Nile. Fortunately for him, Zeus the Thunderer saw him struggling in the water and gave him a fish tail in order to survive. When all danger was past Pan assumed his usual form, but the goat-fish is now the astrological symbol of Capricorn.

#  Typhon

Typhon, the son of Mother Earth, was a terrifying monster. From his thighs downwards he was composed of coiled serpents, a hundred dragons' heads sprung from his shoulders and his body was covered with feathers; thick bristles sprouted from his head and cheeks, and flaming rocks hurtled from his mouth. He was taller than the highest mountain, for his brutish ass-head touched the stars and his vast wings darkened the sky. Typhon symbolized the destructive powers of the volcano, and the volcanic-smelling sirocco bearing his name was personified as an ass by the Egyptians.

When he challenged the Greek Gods, they fled to Egypt in terror. Only Athene stood her ground, and taunted the great Zeus with his cowardice. Stung by her accusations, Zeus responded by casting his thunderbolts at the awesome adversary, and grappled with him; but Typhon was stronger, and wrenched out the sinews of Zeus' hands and feet, leaving him helpless. However, Pan and Hermes retrieved the sinews and restored Zeus to health.

In the following battle, Zeus finally overpowered the monster by interposing thunderbolts between himself and the missiles thrown by his adversary. Typhon then fled to Sicily where Zeus crushed him under Mount Etna and even today his fires belch from its core.

# Cyclops

When the world was created and Mother Earth emerged out of chaos, the three Cyclops Brontes, Steropes and Arges were among her first-born children. The word *cyclops* means 'ring-eyed' or 'eye as big as the full moon' and the Cyclops were so-called because each had only one eye that stared out from the middle of their forehead.

In Homer's *Odyssey*, the Cyclops and their descendants were shepherds living in caves hollowed out of the hillside. Odysseus and his crew stumbled upon one of these caves, entered and were feasting merrily when the owner Polyphemus arrived, driving his sheep before him. When he saw Odysseus and his men, he closed the door with a boulder so large that twenty men could not shift it. Odysseus spoke softly to the monster, reminding him of the duties that a host owes to his guests. This was futile, for not only was Polyphemus dull-witted but also cannibalistic; that night he dashed two of the sailors' brains out on the floor and ate their bodies. In the morning he killed two more sailors and left, shutting the rest of the crew securely in the cave.

During the day, Odysseus found a stake of green olive-wood which he sharpened and hardened. When the Cyclops arrived home, Odysseus offered him a bowl of wine from his own wineskin and again spoke softly to him saying that his name was Oudeis, which means 'nobody'.

'I will save you until last, Oudeis,' promised Polyphemus. Odysseus smiled grimly and offered him more wine.

The Cyclops soon fell into a drunken sleep giving Odysseus and his sailors the opportunity to heat the stake in the fire and drive it into the Cyclops' single eye. Polyphemus screamed for help and the rest of the Cyclops gathered round the cave door outside to find out what had happened.

'I am blind and in pain. Oudeis did it!' he bellowed.

'If nobody is to blame, you must be feverish,' they replied, 'Be quiet,' and returned home.

Polyphemus felt his way to the boulder, rolled it away from the door and stood in front of it waiting to catch the men as they tried to escape. He also touched the backs of his sheep as they went out to pasture, to make sure that no one was astride them. But Odysseus had tied himself and his companions under the bellies of some of the rams and thus escaped.

## Lamia

In Greek mythology, the celebrated beauty Lamia, Queen of Libya, was the secret lover of the God Zeus who, in return for her favours, bestowed on her the peculiar ability to pluck out and replace her eyes at will. She bore a number of children but all of them except Scylla were killed by Hera, the jealous wife of Zeus. Lamia took perverse revenge for having lost her own offspring by destroying the children of others and behaved in such a cruel manner that she was metamorphosed into a wild beast. Her head still remained that of a beautiful enchantress but it was now set upon an animal's body which had the claws of a cat on its front legs and a cow's cloven hooves at the back.

Some ancient writings refer to the Lamia as a woman with a serpentine lower body. This links her with other serpent women like the Winter Snake Goddess and Lilith, the serpentine first wife of Adam who, in medieval occultism, was actually portrayed as the child-sacrificing demon Lamia. The Goddess Hecate, the 'Terrible Mother', the personification of the demonic side of female nature, sometimes also appeared in the form of a Lamia.

## Scylla

*Overleaf*

Scylla, the once beautiful daughter of Lamia and Triton, the Old Man of the Sea, was transformed into a fearful sea-monster by the sorceress Circe, who was jealous of the God Glaucus' love for the nymph. Scylla became an obese brute with twelve misshapen feet and from the lower part of her body grew six hideous dogs with mouths containing a triple row of teeth. She concealed her body in a cave at the bottom of a cliff with her six heads rearing up out of the chasm. Close-by lived Charybdis, a maiden who was transmuted into a whirlpool whose vortex was so strong that it could suck down a ship into the depths of the sea.

In *The Odyssey*, Homer tells of the perils that Odysseus had to face when he and his crew steered their ship between the two cliffs that were the homes of Scylla and Charybdis. Odysseus' ship had to draw close to the cliff where Scylla dwelt, in order to avoid the frightful whirlpool of Charybdis and, as he approached, Scylla shot out of the water, each dog salivating hungrily. They snapped up a number of Odysseus's sailors and ate them with relish, but on that occasion, Odysseus himself escaped unscathed.

# Medusa

The Gorgon Medusa was described as 'the one who killed by the eye by fascination'. In Greek mythology, the Gorgons were three beautiful sisters named Stheno, Eurale and Medusa. The Sea God Poseidon desired the lovely Medusa and, disguised as a horse, lay with her in a temple dedicated to the Goddess Athene. The Goddess was furious that they had desecrated her temple in this fashion and changed Medusa into a fearsome, winged monster.

Originally Medusa was depicted as a horse with wings, then as a woman with equine hindquarters and wings on her hair. At a later date, portraits of her show that her teeth were transformed into the tusks of a wild boar, her tongue protruded, her hands became brazen claws and her wings were changed into serpents. Her staring eyes showed that she had the power to turn men into stone.

It has been suggested that the terrifying face of the Gorgon was derived from Anatolian and Syrian sculptures of attendant lions, which had open mouths and lolling tongues. Medusa was called the Mistress of the West Gate of Death because her home lay at the entrance to the Underworld on the side of the western ocean and she represents the power of the Great Earth Goddess in her most terrible aspect.

It is not certain whether Athene also transformed Medusa's two sisters but in Hesiod's poem *The Shield of Hercules* these two Gorgons were 'not to be approached and not to be described'. On their belts were two writhing serpents and over the terrible heads of these Gorgons a great 'dread' quivered. These two sisters were immortal; only Medusa could die.

The hero Perseus swore a vow to King Polydectes that he would obtain the head of Medusa for the King. Athene, still seeking revenge, decided to aid Perseus by helping him obtain a pair of winged sandals, a helmet of invisibility and a pouch in which he could carry the Gorgons head. Hermes presented the hero with a moon shaped sickle called a harpe and Athene gave him a burnished mirror.

Perseus flew westwards, carried aloft by his winged sandals, to the land of the Hyperboreans where the Gorgons lay sleeping surrounded by the petrified shapes of men and beasts. Perseus, looking only at the reflected image of Medusa in the mirror, struck off her head with a single blow of his harpe.

From out of Medusa's decapitated body sprung the winged horse Pegasus and the warrior Chrysaor. These were the offspring of Medusa and the God Poseidon. Perseus placed Medusa's head in his pouch and made good his escape from Medusa's enraged sisters by wearing the Helmet of Invisibility.

While Perseus was returning across the desert wastes of Libya, drops of blood fell on to the ground from the severed head of Medusa. Mother Earth received these drops and transformed them into venomous serpents of many kinds which is the reason why that particular desert is so infested with snakes. Athene and the healer Aesculapius divided the Gorgon's blood between them. Aesculapius took the blood from her right vein which restored life, and Athene collected the blood from her left vein which brought death and earned for herself the title of 'Instigator of Wars'. Perseus later gave Medusa's head to Athene who fixed it upon her Aegis, or impenetrable shield.

The Medusa's shield of Athene was a favourite theme for armourers and sculptors in ancient times and also in the Renaissance. In ancient Greece oven and kiln doors were similarly embellished with Gorgon masks to frighten away children who could ruin the baking and also hurt themselves by opening these doors.

# Echidne

Chrysaor, the son of Medusa, married Callirhoe who gave birth to the Winter Snake Goddess, Echidne, within a deep, dank cave beneath the earth. Echidne possessed the upper body of a fair-faced nymph with a seductive and alluring manner. Unhappily, her lower half was that of a serpent – terrible, great, spotted and ravenous. She grew up in her cave and used her beautiful head and torso to lure men to her but once they were trapped, her serpent nature took over and she ate them raw.

Echidne mated with the storm god Typhon and her offspring included Cerberus – the guardian of the Underworld, the ever-vigilant dragon Ladon, the Chimera, the many-headed Hydra, and Orthrus, the two-headed hound of Geryon, who mated with his own mother and became the father of the Sphinx, and the Nemean Lion. In Greek mythology, Echidne's role is that of the monstrous mother – devouring and incestuous. She was killed, while she slept, by the hundred-eyed Argus Panoptes.

The serpent woman and her brood were considered to be responsible for much of the hardship and chaos that existed in the world. Christian symbolism turned her into a notorious prostitute whose visible attractions do not conceal her shameful lower nature.

# Minotaur

The Sea God Poseidon, to avenge an insult to him by Minos, King of Crete, caused the King's wife, Pasiphae, to fall passionately in love with a white bull that emerged from the sea. She commissioned Daedalus, the famed Athenian craftsman, to build a hollow wooden cow in which she could conceal herself. The model was so lifelike that the bull mounted it, giving Pasiphae all that she desired. The monster that was born from this unnatural union, the Minotaur, had a calf's head and a human body.

The Minotaur was the living result of Pasiphae's degenerate lust and Minos was determined to conceal her disgrace and his own humiliation. He also turned to Daedalus and instructed him to build an inescapable maze to be called the Labyrinth which, when finished, became the home of the Minotaur. There the Minotaur grew into a fully developed man with the head of a fighting bull bearing a sharp crescent-shaped pair of horns.

In requital for the death of his son Androgeus, King Minos demanded tribute from the Athenians every nine years. He required that seven youths and seven maidens were to be sent to the Cretan Labyrinth, there to become the victims of the ferocious man-eating Minotaur. The hero Theseus was staying in Athens when the tribute fell for the third time. He was determined to end the misery of the people by killing the Minotaur and offered himself in place of one of the sacrificial victims.

When the ship bearing the human sacrifices reached Crete, Minos and his family came down to the harbour to count the youths and maidens. Minos' daughter Ariadne fell in love with Theseus at first sight.

'I will help you to kill my half-brother,' she whispered, 'if you will take me with you as your wife!'

Theseus gladly accepted and she gave him certain instructions. When he entered the Labyrinth, he tied the end of a ball of thread to the doorway and dropped the ball. It rolled downwards, twisting and turning until it reached the Minotaur at the heart of the Labyrinth. Theseus, well armed and agile, was able to kill the unprepared Minotaur and return to the light of day by following the thread.

Ariadne embraced Theseus passionately when he emerged from the Labyrinth and, together with the rest of the Athenians, boarded ship and set sail for their homeland. However, some days later, after disembarking on the island of Dia, the ungrateful Theseus left Ariadne asleep on the shore and quickly sailed away.

# Werewolf

Legends about Werewolves come mainly from Europe, the Balkans and Russia; they set forth stories of one of the most ancient of mankind's superstitions – the metamorphosis of human into wolf. Werewolves were feared in Ancient Greece where lycanthropy – the gradual changing of man into beast – was referred to as *lupinam insanium* which literally means 'wolf madness'; the word lycanthropy itself is derived from the Greek *luk anthropia,* meaning 'wolf man'.

The condition of lycanthropy was one that could strike anyone, anywhere, at any time, although it occurred most often at the time of the full moon. A true Werewolf not only looks like a wolf but also considers him or herself to be one. When the change from human to beast occurs, the features blur and coarsen, the body and palms of the hands become covered with fur, the eyes redden and glow, the nose runs, the mouth salivates, speech is replaced by gutteral sounds and the Werewolf drops to an animal position on all fours with its nails extended into claws.

The lycanthrope is both the villain of his metamorphosis and its victim, for when he returns to human shape the remembrance of the foul murders he has performed while in the form of a wolf will continually haunt him. It is small wonder that, by day, he is stricken with remorse, for the usual way for a Werewolf to kill is by biting through the jugular vein of his victim and feasting on the remains.

The only hope and cure for a Werewolf is death but it can only be destroyed in certain ways. In early times the Werewolf could be dispatched by fire or a sword, but later the most usual way to kill the beast was to shoot it, using a silver bullet – preferably one made from a silver crucifix.

The legends about Werewolves were believed to be totally factual by the people who lived in mountainous and rural districts of Europe, where wolves were a common menace. A dreadful end befell anyone whom the local populace suspected of being a Werewolf. The accused was either burnt alive or beheaded. Sometimes, in order to see if the accusation was true, the suspect Werewolf was cut open to see if there was fur was on the inside of its skin, as many people believed that a Werewolf could reverse its skin in order to avoid recognition.

# Formorians

The Formorians of Ireland were a malignant race of giants. The bodies of these uncouth demons were composed of a diverse collection of twisted human and animal flesh; some had animal bodies and human heads, some had only one arm or leg, and some were piscine with webbed feet and human features. Not one could lay any claim to beauty.

These Formori were believed to have existed from before the Great Flood and were skilled in the magical arts. Their leader was King Conan, but it was his malignant deputy Balor who had the most sinister reputation. Balor's single eye was invested with so much venomous power that it took the strength of four men to lift his eyelid. Most of the time he kept his eye closed but when the tribe needed help, his servants would lift his eyelid and all who met his gaze died instantly.

The Formorians were a warlike people who fought off anyone who tried to wrest their country from them. Partholan and his people all died in their attempt at this when the Formori used their magical arts to inflict a form of deadly plague upon them.

Eventually the Fir Bolga, Irish refugees returning from Greece, subdued the Formori and managed to coexist peaceably with them. They, in turn however, were conquered by a new brave race armed with golden spears and helmets, the Tuatha de Danaan, who slaughtered the entire community of Formorians.

# Grendel

In the Anglo-Saxon poem *Beowulf*, the Scylding King Hrothgar reigned over the people of Denmark in great splendour and built a magnificent new home, Heorot Hall, for himself and his courtiers. However, the day it was finished a great calamity befell the very first banquet held there. Grendel, a living fiend and gruesome prowler of the borderland, came stalking them. Time and again he forced entry into the hall, leaving behind the mangled, half-eaten bodies of Hrothgar's warriors, strewn among the debris on the rush floor. Those that were left standing fled for their lives across the land of Denmark, leaving the great hall empty.

In the land of the Geats, the strongest man alive, Beowulf, heard of the bitter sorrows of the Danes and felt so much compassion for their plight that he turned to his men and gave the order,

'Get my ship ready. The Danish King needs us!'

King Hrothgar was overjoyed to see the great warrior and glad to accept his offer to exterminate the monster. He took the Geatish warriors to Heorot Hall and set a great feast before them.

'This night,' he said to Beowulf, 'stand in my stead. Uphold me, and you shall be richly rewarded.' The King, his Queen and his Earls left the hall, and the great warrior and his men remained behind to wait for the monster.

Then from across the dark moors, Grendel came, wet and slimy from his home in the lake. He burst open the doors of the hall and surveyed the Geatish warriors asleep on their fur beds. Rolling his monstrous head from side to side, red light shot from his deep-set eyes. He laughed with satisfaction at the sight.

Beowulf was not asleep; his cold, calm eyes followed every move of Grendel as the demon pulled one of the warriors to him, ripped the man's body apart with his talons and drunk his hot blood. Grendel dropped the torn remains of the warrior and moved on to Beowulf. As Grendel rushed at him, Beowulf caught the demon by the arm and tightened his grip. When Grendel felt the power of the warrior, he was sorely afraid and tried to escape but was unable to do so for Beowulf twisted the ogre's arm right round his back. Grendel's screams of agony aroused Beowulf's squire who up until then, had been paralysed with horror; he tried to stab the monster with his sword, but blow after blow fell on the Ogre's tough hide without leaving a scratch. No tool made by man had any power against Grendel.

But Beowulf had not yet exerted all his strength; he suddenly wrenched Grendel's arm even further back, right out of its socket; the bones parted, the muscles tore, the skin broke and Beowulf was left with the arm of the monster who fled shrieking into the darkness of the lake, there to die. In celebration of this deed, Beowulf hung the bloody arm of Grendel from the rafters of the hall.

# Herne the Hunter

Who would dare wander alone at dusk, through the ancient forest of Windsor Great Park, to turn from the path into deep woodland and there confront the ghost of Herne the Hunter, mounted on a black horse and followed by a pack of hounds? The phantom, surrounded by an eerie blue light, only possesses a slight resemblance to a human being, for he wears the antlered skull of a stag on his head and is draped in a deer's skin.

In the legends of England, Herne was a royal huntsman to King Henry VIII. While hunting in the forest, Herne saved the life of the king by throwing himself between an enraged wounded stag and his master. As he lay on the ground sorely maimed, a sorcerer appeared and commanded that the stag's horns were to be cut off and bound to Herne's forehead. Herne recovered and enjoyed the king's favour but not for long. Favouritism breeds jealousy, and the other huntsmen eventually persuaded the king to dismiss Herne from his service. In despair, the hunter went out into the forest and hung himself from a mighty oak.

His ghost was first seen by the Earl of Surrey while Henry VIII was still on the throne, and Shakespeare mentioned Herne in *The Merry Wives of Windsor*:

> *There is an old tale goes, that Herne the Hunter,*
> *Sometime a keeper here in Windsor Forest,*
> *Doth all the winter time, at still midnight,*
> *Walk round about an oak, with great ragg'd horns;*
> *And there he blasts the trees, and takes the cattle,*
> *And makes milch-kine yield blood, and shakes a chain*
> *In a most hideous and dreadful manner...*

However, the story of Herne was already 'an old tale' in Shakespeare's time, and Herne was associated with the park long before royalty came to Windsor. The 'Wild Hunt' is a common theme in European legends. The shadowy Gwyn ap Nudd, Celtic Warden of the Underworld accompanied by his Gabriel Ratchet Hounds – the Hounds of Hell – would chase the souls of the damned across the stormy skies at night; just to hear the sound of his horn meant certain death.

On black or stormy nights, the Norse God Odinn – also known in the Anglo-Saxon period as Woden – sat astride his eight-legged steed Sleipnir with his hounds at his heels, and would lead his wild army of the homeless dead across the sky; whole trees were bent aside with the force of their passing. It is said that if the hunt catches a mortal, that person is instantly transported to another place, but has to remain silent about the huntsman or face death.

Herne's antlers, in all probability, identify him with Cernunnos, the horned Celtic fertility god. Margaret Murray, in her book *The God of the Witches* says,

'The great Gaulish god was called by the Romans Cernunnos which in English parlance was Herne or more colloquially 'Old Hornie' – an apt name for a fertility god. Windsor Forest may well have been the site of one of Cernunnos's ancient shrines where the trees themselves would form his temple.'

According to legend, when England is in crisis, the phantom of Herne will appear on a jet-black horse, silhouetted against the sky, with his hounds at his heels. But a crisis is not always necessary, for his latest appearance was reputedly in 1962, when a group of youngsters found a hunting horn in the forest and without thinking, blew it. Immediately another horn answered their call followed by the baying of hounds; then, with his antlers branching out from his head, Herne appeared. The terrified youths fled, throwing the horn away in panic.

# Chapter 4 ANIMALS

In the procession of strange creatures that parade through the myths and Bestiaries, none are more exotic than the animals. Often, three or more animal parts, totally diverse, are combined to form a single creature. The Manticore has a lion's body, a human face, a scorpion's tail and a triple row of teeth, whilst the Yale, which is goat-like, has the tusks of a boar, the feet of a unicorn, a spotted skin and folding horns.

Animals are usually considered to be earthbound creatures with all four feet, paws, pads or hooves firmly upon the ground, but not when they are fabulous. The horse Pegasus flies up to Olympus powered by his great wings, and the Hippogryph can also fly aloft while the Golden Ram wings his way to earth.

Animals are quite evidently creatures of understanding and intelligence, and even those with less of these abilities have been so elevated and exploited that, while still retaining their natural shape, the imagery surrounding them can make them seem fabulous. A good example can be found in India where the humble cow is greatly revered as a sacred beast. Sometimes, the division between reality and the fantastic can be very narrow indeed.

*'Twas brillig, and the slithy toves*
*Did gyre and gimble in the wabe...'*
Lewis Carroll, *Through the Looking Glass*

# Griffin

The Griffin can trace its origins back to the Near East where it appears on seal impressions. It was known in Egypt before 3300 BC and is possibly more ancient still. Paintings of this composite beast were also popular in the Minoan and Mycenean Empires. In appearance, the Griffin had the foreparts of an eagle, and the rear, tail and hindlegs of a lion; its eagle-like head had pointed, upstanding ears like those of an ass. Feathers grew upon its head, neck and chest and the rest of the Griffin's body was covered in leonine fur, subtly coloured in shades of tawny brown. Aelian said that the wings of Griffins were white and their necks were variegated in colour with blue feathers. The Griffin's claws were especially valuable as they were reputed to change colour in the presence of poison, which is why they made useful drinking vessels.

There are a number of different types of Griffin; the Snake-Griffin has a lion's body, a snake's head and a bird's legs, and the Lion-Griffin is lion-like but has hind legs shaped like those of a bird. These two types of Griffin were known in Babylonia and appeared in Hittite, Assyrian and Persian art.

Herodotus of Halicarnassus, said that the legends of Griffins came from the Issedonians, who lived beyond the Ural mountains. The Griffins were said to be guardians of hidden treasure and in particular the vast gold mines of India and Scythia. Even their nests in the mountains, where the females laid eggs made of agate, were lined with gold. They would punish humans for their love of gold and other treasures of the earth. The Arimaspians, a bold, one-eyed race of humans, constantly tried to steal their treasure and eventually drove the Griffins away from the mountains.

The blending of two solar creatures, the lion and the eagle, shows that the Griffin is beneficent. They are the sacred beasts of the sun and represent its golden wealth. Griffins drew the chariots of Apollo the Sun God, and Nemesis who personified 'divine vengeance'. The Griffin was particularly sacred to Nemesis, as it had the reputation of being both vengeful and watchful.

The symbolism of the medieval Griffin was ambivalent. It could stand for the Devil but was usually an emblem of Christ. In heraldry, when the Griffin represents Christ, the colour of the eagle half of the beast is golden to signify divinity, and the lion part is flesh pink to signify Christ's human nature.

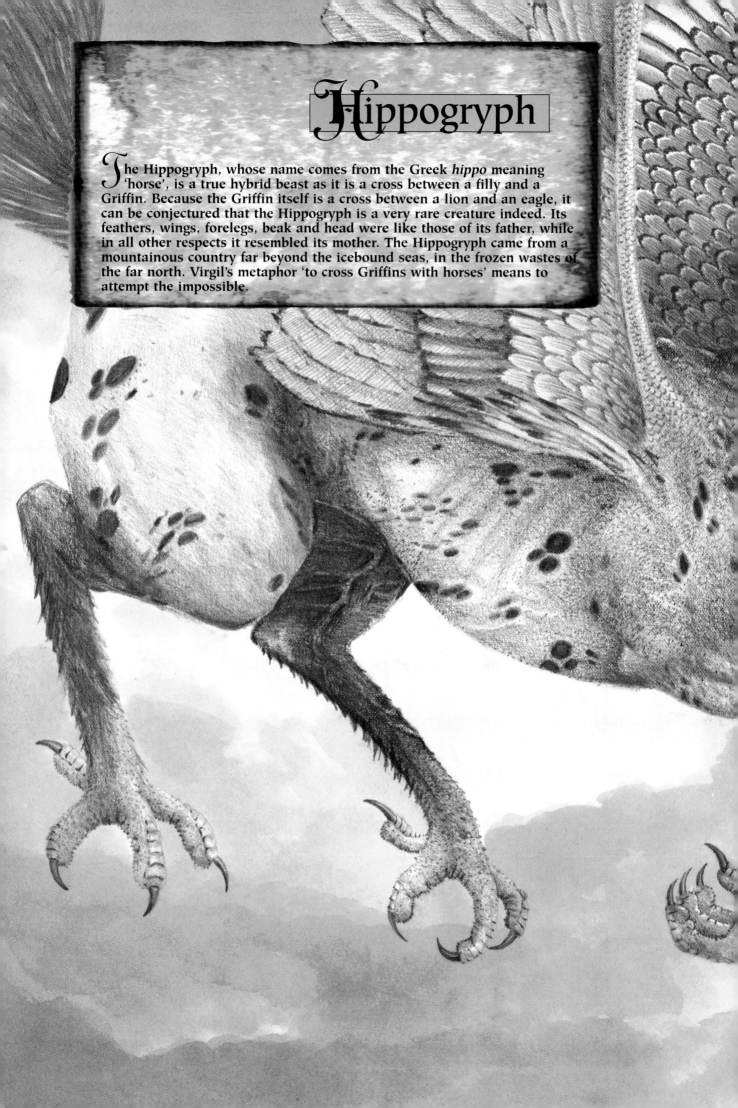

# Hippogryph

The Hippogryph, whose name comes from the Greek *hippo* meaning 'horse', is a true hybrid beast as it is a cross between a filly and a Griffin. Because the Griffin itself is a cross between a lion and an eagle, it can be conjectured that the Hippogryph is a very rare creature indeed. Its feathers, wings, forelegs, beak and head were like those of its father, while in all other respects it resembled its mother. The Hippogryph came from a mountainous country far beyond the icebound seas, in the frozen wastes of the far north. Virgil's metaphor 'to cross Griffins with horses' means to attempt the impossible.

In the sixteenth century, the Italian poet Ariosto used this blend of the Griffin and the winged horse as one of the protagonists in his poem *Orlando Furioso*.

This 'spiritual mount' was the property of the enchanter Atlantes who found that it was awe-inspiring to look at but quite impossible to ride. Atlantes tamed it at last, but in such a way that the fiery beast would answer only to his commands. He taught it to take him anywhere on earth or in heaven.

After Atlantes had been vanquished, the creature became the mount of Atlantes' foster son, Rogero, who had a magical bridle which calmed the Hippogryph. Mounted upon the beast, he travelled the world, rescuing maidens, destroying Harpies and visiting Heaven. Finally, Astolpho, an English Prince, claimed the Hippogryph and set it free.

# Europa and the Bull

When Zeus sent Hermes to drive Agenor's cattle down to the seashore at Tyre, Hermes smiled quietly to himself for he was sure that Zeus was in pursuit of yet another maiden. He was, of course, quite right. Zeus had fallen in love with Europa, Agenor's daughter and she and her companions would walk daily on that very seashore where the cattle now grazed.

Zeus transformed himself into a majestic snow-white bull with great dewlaps and small gem-like horns, and joined the other cattle by the side of the sea. When the great bull wandered up to her, Europa was alarmed; but he was so gentle and friendly that she soon forgot her fear and began to play with him, putting flowers in his mouth and hanging daisy chains around his neck.

Zeus was enchanted; he lay down and allowed her to stroke him and eventually climb on to his broad shoulders. He arose and ambled down to the sea with Europa still seated on his back and, before the maiden realized what was happening, he dove swiftly into deep water, and all that she could do was to look back at the receding shoreline in terror and cling tightly to one of his horns.

Zeus waded ashore at Cretian Gortyna, changed his shape into that of an eagle and ravished Europa under the shade of a great plane tree. She bore him three sons; Minos, Rhadamanthys and Sarpedon.

# Pegasus

When Perseus decapitated the gorgon Medusa, she was already pregnant by the sea god Poseidon who had visited her in the form of a stallion. As her body fell to the ground, the two offspring of this union, Pegasus and the warrior Chrysaor leapt fully developed from her body. Pegasus was a white stallion with a silky mane and golden wings. His warm breath smelt of wild flowers. He was a lunar animal and represented one of the aspects of the Great Goddess when, as the Mareheaded Mother, she was known as Leucippe, the white mare.

Pegasus instantly took flight when he first saw the sky above him; he rode the wind effortlessly as his golden wings carried him to Mount Helicon, the home of the Muses. Pegasus had the ability to cause a fountain of water to gush out wherever he stamped his moon-shaped hoof, and his name actually means 'of the wells'. He created a fountain, known as 'The Horse Well', for the Muses at Hippocrene. The waters conferred poetical inspiration on all who drunk there and Pegasus is also the inspiration of those who strive to perfect their poetic gifts.

The hero Belleraphon had been given the task of killing the evil Chimera and needed the help of Pegasus. He caught the magical horse by throwing a golden bridle, a present from the Goddess Athene, over Pegasus' head while the stallion was drinking at Peirene, another of his wells. This caused the wild horse to become tame and obedient, and he willingly flew his master to the lair of the Chimera. The lithe stallion was much more agile than the ungainly monster and enabled Belleraphon to kill the beast by evading its blasts of flame.

The hero was so elated by his success that he vaingloriously rode Pegasus aloft to Olympus to claim a place amongst the Gods. Zeus was furious at his presumption and sent a gadfly to sting Pegasus under his tail. Pegasus reared, flinging Belleraphon back to earth again, but completed his flight to Olympus where Zeus now uses him to carry his thunderbolts.

In the state religion of Rome, Pegasus was reputed to bear the Emperor on his back to the 'Land of the Dead' and images of Pegasus can be found on many Roman tombstones. The winged horse is symbolic of the combination of higher and lower natures, and of striving to achieve the higher.

# Nemean Lion

When the Goddess Hera, who was vexed by Heracles' excesses, drove him mad, Heracles murdered six of his sons and two of his nephews. He was overwhelmed with remorse when he recovered his sanity and travelled to the Oracle at Delphi, seeking to atone for his sins. The Pythoness advised Heracles to serve King Eurystheus, a man far inferior to himself, for twelve years and perform whatever labours might be set for him; his payment would be immortality.

The First Labour to be imposed on Heracles was to kill and flay the Nemean Lion, the offspring of Typhon and Echidne. Another story of its origins says that Selene, the Goddess of the Moon, created the lion from sea foam, and Iris, the Goddess of the Rainbow, bound it with her girdle, carried it to earth and left it on Mount Tretus near Nemea. The savage creature preyed upon the inhabitants of Nemea and had depopulated the entire area by the time that Heracles appeared on the scene.

The hero first espied the lion returning to its lair on Mount Tretus, blood-stained from the day's slaughter. He shot a quiverful of arrows at it, but the lion's pelt was so thick that they rebounded harmlessly. The lion yawned and licked the blood off its chops. Heracles whirled his great club around his head and dealt the beast an almighty blow on its muzzle. The lion entered its cave shaking its head a little because it had a slight singing in the ears. Heracles shrugged ruefully as he looked at his shattered club; he was now aware that only his great strength could overcome the beast – weapons were useless.

He cast a strong net over one of the two entrances to the cave and went in by the other. Unable to escape, the lion leapt at him; Heracles seized it by the throat and began to squeeze. The lion managed to bite off one of his fingers but Heracles did not relinquish his hold. He continued to constrict the animal's windpipe until it choked to death and then set about flaying the lion by using the creature's own razor-sharp claws as a knife to cut the skin from the flesh. Thereafter he wore the invulnerable pelt as armour and the head as a helmet.

The Twelve Labours of Heracles are considered to be mythological interpretations of the tasks that had to be performed by a candidate for kingship before he could ascend the throne. Indeed, in Greece, Babylon and Syria, the Sacred King's ritual combat with wild beasts was part of the coronation ritual.

# Ceryneian Hind

*I*n some fairy tales, kings have chased a deer through enchanted
forests, often to give up before capturing their quarry. The chase of
the hind or roebuck represents the pursuit of wisdom and, symbolically,
the Third Labour of Heracles is an example of this search to obtain
knowledge. He had to capture the Ceryneian Hind from the grove of
Artemis at Ceryneia and bring her unharmed to Mycenae. This task was
of a different order from most of his other labours for he could not use
even the least force. Instead he had to exercise patience and gentleness.

The Ceryneian Hind was a swift, dappled creature, larger than a bull,
shod with bronze and crowned with golden horns like those of a stag.
When the Goddess Artemis was a child, she saw five of these hinds on
the banks of the river Anaurus. She caught four and harnessed them to
her chariot; the fifth fled to Ceryneia.

Heracles was not allowed to harm the hind and chased her as far as
Istria and the land of the Hyperboreans. For a whole year he hunted her
until, exhausted, she took refuge on Mount Artemisium. Heracles took
careful aim and let fly an arrow which pinned her forelegs together; the
arrow passed between bone and sinew and drew not one drop of blood.
Heracles was then able to lay her across his shoulders and bring her
back to Mycenae.

# Erymanthian Boar

The boar is the symbol of strength, fearlessness and savagery; it is the untamed creature of the wood and, because of its crescent-shaped tusks, is also sacred to the Moon. In Greek mythology, the Fourth Labour that Eurystheus set for Heracles was to capture alive the Erymanthian Boar – a beast as black as night, with flaming red eyes and tusks longer than a man's arm – and bring it back to Mycenae.

This ferocious animal haunted the cypress-covered slopes of Mount Erymanthus and all the surrounding countryside, killing humans and animals indiscriminately. Mount Erymanthus was named after a son of Apollo, blinded by Aphrodite because he had seen her bathing. In retribution, Apollo transformed himself into a boar and tore Aphrodite's lover Adonis to pieces. Yet Mount Erymanthus is sacred to Artemis, the Moon Goddess who carries a silver bow.

It was winter when Heracles set out and the snow-drifts were deep, so the easiest way to travel was by boat. Heracles rowed along the river Erymanthus looking for any signs of the boar and thought, 'This is a tricky undertaking but, although the beast is large, its brain is small. It should be easy enough to outwit it!' Heracles planned his strategy carefully, he stalked the boar and found it hiding in a thicket. Adjusting his position so that a snow-drift was between him and the boar, he gave a loud 'Halloo'. The startled boar shot out of its hide to attack him and ran straight into the snowdrift. This was just what Heracles hoped would happen; he jumped upon its back, bound it with chains and carried it back to the city.

Earlier, King Eurystheus, who was finding Heracles' displays of power and strength rather overwhelming, commanded his smiths to forge a great bronze urn, which they buried underground. Whenever Heracles returned from one of his labours, the King would take refuge in the urn and send his herald to announce the details of Heracles' next task.

It was just as well that he had hidden himself on this occasion, for Heracles deposited the boar alive and kicking, despite its chains, in the market place and set off to join Jason and his Argonauts who were gathering for their voyage to Colchis. Nobody knows who eventually killed the boar but its tusks were once to be seen in the temple of Apollo at Cumae.

# Cerberus

Cerberus was the watchdog of the Underworld, who guarded the souls of the dead and prevented their return to the world above. This offspring of the storm god Typhon and the serpent Echidne had a tail bristling with serpents' heads, a dragon's back and a great number of heads. Hesiod, in his *Theogony*, wrote that Cerberus had fifty heads; Pindar and Horace said that he had a hundred, but he is usually illustrated with three. The three heads relate to the threefold symbols of the baser forces of life; they are the infernal replica of the divine trinity, or it may be that they represent past, present and the time yet to come. Dante described Cerberus as *'il gran vermo inferno'* thus linking him with the legendary worms and orms.

At the gates of the Underworld, Cerberus would be offered honey cakes – 'a sop to Cerberus' – by the souls of the dead to ensure their safe passage. He would welcome them with a wagging tail but tear to pieces any who tried to escape.

The Twelfth and last Labour of Heracles was his 'Harrowing of Hell' where he had to capture Cerberus in the House of Hades, on the banks of the Stygian lake and drag him into the land of the living. He succeeded in binding Cerberus with adamantine chains, and hauled him up a subterranean path from the Underworld; barking furiously, his slaver dripped from his jaws upon the ground, and wherever it fell there grew the poisonous plant Aconite.

# Golden Ram

Phrixus, the son of the Boeotian King Athamus, was so hated by his stepmother Ino that she plotted a unique method of engineering his death. Ino organised a catastrophic crop failure by persuading the women of Boeotia to parch the corn without their husbands' knowledge. The Queen knew that this would cause her husband to send a message to the Oracle at Delphi asking for advice. She then bribed the messenger to say that the only way that the land could be fertile again was for Athamus to sacrifice Phrixus.

The Gods in Olympus were horrified at her wickedness and Hermes sent a winged Golden Ram to the prince's rescue. The Ram was able to fly, talk and prophesy the future. It flew to Phrixus' side just as Athamus, grieving bitterly, was on the point of slitting Phrixus' throat.

'Climb on my back!' the Ram commanded, and the youth obeyed.

'Take me too,' pleaded his sister Helle, 'for there is no safety here.' Phrixus pulled his sister up behind him and the Ram flew high into the sky, heading for the land of Colchis.

Unfortunately the height and speed of the Ram's flight began to affect Helle. She became dizzy, lost her hold and fell to her death in the straits between Europe and Asia, which today are called Hellespont in her honour. The Ram carried Phrixus safely to Colchis where he considered that it was his duty to sacrifice the gleaming beast to Zeus the Deliverer.

The Ram's golden fleece became famous a generation later when Jason and his Argonauts set out in their ship Argo, on a quest to bring the golden fleece home from Colchis. After facing many dangers and adventures, Jason at last reached his destination but his request to be given the fleece was met by King Aeetes with a savage refusal; he also threatened to cut out Jason's tongue and cut off his head.

However, the God of Love aimed one of his arrows at Aeetes' daughter Medea, compelling her to fall head over heels in love with Jason. In return for Jason's promise to keep faith with her forever, Medea led Jason to the precinct of Ares. There the fleece hung on an oak tree, guarded by an immortal dragon coiled a thousand times around the tree. Now, Medea was an enchantress and had no fear of dragons; she soothed it with incantations and, using freshly cut sprigs of juniper, shook a sleeping draught onto his eyelids. The dragon was soon deeply asleep. Jason quickly unfastened the fleece and the pair fled to where the Argo lay at anchor. Eventually Jason hung the fleece in the Temple of Laphystian Zeus in Boeotian Orchomenus.

# Manticore

Pliny described the Manticore as a blood-red creature, having the body of a lion, the face and ears of an azure-eyed human, a long neck, and a tail ending in a sting like that of a scorpion. The mouth of a Manticore contains a triple row of teeth which fit alternately into each other and are vicious to behold. Its voice is shrill and resembles the combined sound of the flute and trumpet, although it can also hiss like a serpent. The sturdy legs of the Manticore are so powerful that, when it leaps into the air, no place can contain it; no other creature can outpace the monster for it can run faster than even any bird can fly. It can shoot out the quills of its tail like darts which spread all around for a great distance.

The Manticore is one of the most dangerous beasts known to the human race, for not only is it impossible to capture, but it also loves to eat human flesh. This is probably why its name, derived from the Persian, means 'man-eater'.

In Romanesque decorations, the Manticore is more often portrayed with female features and wears a type of Phrygian cap; she may be compared with Sirens and other dangerous monsters.

# Peryton

In the sixteenth century, a rabbi found a fragment of a treatise from the Alexandrian library. It contained information about the savage Peryton who lived in China and was believed to have originated in Atlantis. These creatures were half-deer and half-bird – combining the body, strong wings and green-coloured plumage of a bird, with the head, antlers and legs of a deer. If its antlers were damaged, they would immediately regrow.

The Peryton was even more unusual in that instead of casting a shadow of its own body when the sun shone, it cast the shadow of a man. This aspect of the creature made the superstitious think that the Peryton was the spirit of a wanderer who had died when away from home. However, the Peryton, almost as if denying this, was the mortal foe of the human race for it believed that its own shadow would return to it only if it succeeded in killing a man. A Peryton would swoop to earth, entangle a man in its antlers and carry him high into the sky before dropping its victim to his death.

A story is told of how a wing of Perytons swooped down on the ships of those who came to conquer Carthage, killing and wounding the soldiers indiscriminately. No weapon was known that could kill a Peryton and the only thing that saved the army was the fact that a Peryton can only kill one person at a time.

# Water Horses

Goborchinu are Irish Horse-heads; Afanc is the Welsh name for them; the Endrop is the Rumanian version and in Scotland they are called Kelpies or Highland Water Horses. These fabulous amphibians can be divided into two types: horses of the sea, often called Hippocamps, whose powers over the water are controlled by a higher authority, and lake or river horses who are demonic.

The Sea Horse is portrayed with the head, foreparts and front legs of a horse co-joined to the lower half of the body and tail of a fish. Sea Horses are the steeds of the sea gods and of night, and represent the humid element, lunar power, fertility and chaos. They draw the chariot of the Greek god Poseidon, controller of the sea, earthquakes and springs; he is said to have created the horse and is regarded as an equestrian deity. The blind forces of primordial chaos can be symbolized by the Hippocamps that are driven and controlled by Poseidon's trident.

Some Sea Horses are not composite creatures. The thirteenth-century cosmographer Zakariyya al-Qaswini wrote in his treatise *Wonders of Creation* that the Sea Horse is like the horse of dry land, but its mane and its tail grow longer; its colour is more lustrous and its hooves are cleft like those of wild oxen. These superb creatures lived in the sea but would emerge to mate with any mare tethered near the water. Zakariyya al-Qaswini also stated that the resultant offspring of this mating was very beautiful; one foal of this crossbreeding was said to be dark with white spots like pieces of silver.

Water Horses who live in lakes and fresh water are very often seen in a sinister light as they are fearsome monsters that are kin to the Nixies, malignant Slavonic water demons. The Kelpie is perhaps the most notorious example of a water demon – every lake in Scotland is reputed to have one – but it is difficult to identify them for they are shape-shifters capable of assuming a number of forms.

When the Kelpie appears in horse form, it is a splendid young steed, black and wild of eye. It looks just like an ordinary horse except for one small feature, it has backwards pointing hooves with the tuft on the pastern reversed; its footprints are unmistakeable. A Kelpie, wearing a bridle, will wait by the side of a river until a weary traveller sees it, mounts and tries to ride away. It then throws up its head, dives into deep water and disappears, leaving its rider to swim or drown. Yet someone who knows the wiles of a Kelpie can overcome it. The trick is to exchange its own bridle for an ordinary one and the Kelpie will become quite tame and do all the tasks that its master sets for it. But it should not be kept for too long or it will curse its captor and his descendants forever.

Sometimes the Kelpie appears in human form. A man quietly riding his horse along a river bank will suddenly and fearfully become aware that someone is sitting behind him. Then two hairy arms encircle him, clamping his body close to its own, crushing the very breath out of its victim. The man loses control of his horse which gallops wildly along the waterside; the hairy visitant eventually gets tired of the sport and vanishes. Perhaps a lass sitting by the side of a lake will see a handsome young man appear out of the water with waterweed or shells in his hair. He holds out beckoning arms to her, enticing her to him in the water, to drown in his arms.

Another Scottish Water Demon was the Ech-Ushkya (in Gaelic, *Each-uisge*). It was a handsome horse or pony that stood by the waterside waiting for some unsuspecting person to catch and ride it. That was the last action that its dupe took, however, for the Ech-Ushkya was impossible to dismount and the man-eating fiend left only a portion of its victim's body, washed up on the shore, to show what had happened to it.

# Yale

One fabulous beast that is seen most often in heraldry is the Yale, which is also known as the Eale, and the Jall. It is described as being as big as a horse, goat-like – *Ya-el* means mountain goat in Hebrew – with teeth like a boar, the feet of a unicorn, spots of various colours and a self-satisfied expression. The Yale is reputed to be able to adjust its outlandishly long horns, folding one back when it is fighting so as to have one sharp weapon ready when needed.

The Yale was described by Pliny the Elder, who said that it was the size of a hippopotamus with the jaws of a boar, an elephant's tail, movable horns and was coloured black or tawny.

The Yale that is portrayed in the art of Southern India also has an elephant's tail together with a boar's head and a goat-like beard. It too had swivelling horns which made it an excellent protector, and effigies of it were used as temple guardians to ward off evil spirits.

In the heraldry of England, the Yale is one of Queen Elizabeth II's beasts. These are a set of carved animals that illustrate, with heraldic emblems, the Queen's royal ancestry. One of the sculptures of the royal beasts at Hampton Court Palace is the Yale of Beaufort and represents the House of Lancaster.

# Fenrir

Nearly everything that we know about the mythology of the Scandinavian people comes from the Icelandic 'Edda' texts. The *Prose Edda* was compiled in the thirteenth century by an historian named Snorri Sturluson who recounted the story of the wolf Fenrir – the son of the mischief-making God Loki – who was brother to both Midgard's Worm and Death himself.

The Wolf caused so much trouble that the High Gods decided to shackle him to a rock in the Underworld. This was a difficult feat, for Fenrir was so huge that his jaws stretched from Heaven to Earth. The great beast easily broke the first two bonds with which the Gods tried to hold him, but the third was different. Its name was Gleipnir and it had been created by a dwarf from the Land of the Dark Elves and was forged from a woman's beard, the noise of a cat's footstep, the roots of a mountain, the breath of a fish, the nerves of a bear and a bird's spittle. Fenrir refused to be bound with this rope unless one of the Gods put his hand between his jaws. Tyr agreed and put his hand in position. Fenrir bit off Tyr's hand but the rope held and the wolf was bound firmly. The captive opened his mouth wide in rage, trying to savage anyone who came near, so the Gods wedged a sword between his jaws with the pommel at his bottom jaw and the point transfixing his palate. There he lay until Ragnarok – the battle that caused the end of the world.

Eventually the great terror of the Ragnarok came, heralded by a great winter that lasted three years. Fenrir snapped the bonds that anchored him and advanced to war against the Gods. Night fell over the world as another wolf called Skoll captured and devoured the Sun. Fenrir joined forces with the other evil entities – Loki, Garm the Hound of Hell, and Midgard's Worm – to battle against the Gods. Fenrir swallowed the mighty God Odinn, the other High Gods perished and fire consumed the Earth. However there was a small ray of hope left after this holocaust because some of the younger sons of the Gods survived. Odinn's son Vidar eventually slew Fenrir by tearing the creature apart, Earth revived and a new cycle of life began.

Nordic mythology surmises that it is only possible to bring about order by temporarily binding the chaotic and destructive powers of evil. Fenrir appears in the myths as the symbol of these forces.

# Sleipnir

The Norse God Odinn was identified by
the two ravens Huginn and Muninn, or
'Thought' and 'Memory', that he carried on
his shoulder, and his eight-legged stallion,
Sleipnir. Odinn, as the leader of the Wild
Hunt, rode his steed Sleipnir across the
dark stormy sky at night, at the head of his
host of dead warriors. Farmers would leave
their last sheaf of grain for Sleipnir hoping
that the hunt would pass by without
injuring them, for it was the hunt of death
and people could be swept up in it and
carried away.

It is possible that both Odinn and his
steed had the same origins, together
personifying the powers of darkness and
death. A carving on a gravestone from
Tjangride in Gothland shows a man riding
on an eight-legged horse and either
represents Odinn riding his horse Sleipnir,
or figures a dead man being carried away
by the Horse God.

Odinn was also a shaman, a priest or
psychopomp who cured sickness, directed
sacrifice and escorted the souls of the dead
to the other world. The shaman has a close
affinity with horses because he himself will
sacrifice a horse offered to the Gods and in
spirit escort the animal's soul aloft. He
obtains admission to the higher planes in
this way, to seek aid for the community
which he serves. Sleipnir, as Odinn's steed,
draws attention to the shaman's powers of
sending his soul in swift flight to heaven.

Sleipnir not only carried the dead to
heaven; he was also capable of travelling
to the underworld where Hel reigns.

When Balder the Beautiful suffered a
bloody death as a result of Loki's spite,
Frig, Odinn's wife, spoke up. 'Who is there
who will earn our undying gratitude by
riding down the road to Hel and asking if
she will accept a ransom for Balder?'

Hermod the Swift strode forward,
Sleipnir was led from his stable and the
two galloped away.

Hermod rode for nine days and nine
nights down ravines, each one getting
darker and deeper, until he came to the
hall of Hel. The Queen of the Underworld
said that she would set a test to see if it
was true that Balder was so beloved. If
only one thing on earth refused to mourn,
Balder must stay with her.

Hermod rode Sleipnir back to Frig and,
at once, she asked everything to mourn.
Humans and beasts, earth, stones and
trees all complied with her request – except
one. It was of course Loki the
Mischiefmaker who refused to honour
Balder with his grief, and so he remained
in Hel's domain.

# Index